RULE NO. 1 – A SATISFIED CUSTOMER . . .

'Will you be very long, Jonny?' asked Miss Prendergastly.
'About the usual length.'
'And what is that?'
'A secret between my conscience and the ballot-box,' I reply.
She sits there, swinging her long legs, smiling at me. I notice that the more she swings, the more I can see. Those beautiful thighs, ending in the white vee of . . . Just a gosh-darned minute!
I'll be hornswoggled if she hasn't changed her undies. Now she seems . . . I stare harder . . . to be wearing a pair of fur frillies! I can see so fur and no farther. She must be expecting a road accident, I tell myself . . .

Also in the Confessions Series and available from Sphere Books:

Confessions Of A Gasman

JONATHAN MAY

SPHERE BOOKS LIMITED
30/32 Gray's Inn Road, London WC1X 8JL

Published in Great Britain by Sphere Books Ltd, 1977

The dedications to all of you who've written in with your nice comments, jokes, birthday cards and, last but not least, the frillies, are a couple of pages further on.

Apart from that, this book is also for Helen, Charlie, Catherine and Theresa. They're nice people and I'm glad that they're among my friends.

TRADE
MARK

Set in Intertype Plantin

Printed in Great Britain by
Hunt Barnard Printing Ltd.,
Aylesbury, Bucks.

Contents

DEDICATIONS

You'll notice that it's getting shorter.

The Dedications pages is what I'm talking about, folks. This is partly because my Publisher didn't like it being so long, and again I'm talking about the Dedications. I'm also talking about something that makes my Publisher envious, but that is by the way. Also, I have closed my joke competition and I think this might have put some of you off writing. Anyway, for those of you who have been in touch with me, thanks a lot.

First, the winner of the competition.

Who else?

Ann Summers of Aylesbury. Nothing is too good for the lady. Or should that be no *thing* is too good? Anyway, over the last couple of years she has kept me fascinated by an endless stream of jokes, with the odd frilly to mop off my brow. And some of her frillies are very odd indeed. But she has been amazing and I am truly grateful.

Among the honourable mentions is the lovely Pandora, who keeps dragging drawers from her bottom drawer in such profusion that I fear for her nether regions when the weather turns really cold.

And to everyone else who sent in jokes and frillies, a big thanks. I got a lot out of the jokes and thought a lot about what used to be in the frillies. If any of you have still got any that need clearing out, then throw them my way.

All the way from Fiji, my thanks go to Kalara Saleleyawa.

I hope that Trooper Mick Waters from the Fifth Dragoon Guards is still enjoying guard duty.

I don't know if Pam Arrumm is still a pupil at the Bishop Douglas School in London, but if she is then I think she's a credit to the place. Wish I'd been Games Master there instead of where I finished up. (Plug for *Confessions Of A Games Master*.)

Thanks also to Margaret Fletcher who lives near Ludlow. Nice ones, Margaret.

And R. L. Doeve from Holland. All I'm missing now is the little Dutch cap. He mentions some of his friends, and I'm sure that they've been dedicated in earlier books of mine. As I haven't got any copies left I'll just have to put them in again. Anyway, I rather enjoy putting them in again, don't you Missus? They're Julie (Super-cook) Doeve, Juliana (Into-everything) Doeve, Mick (Super-chocks) Tozer, Linda (Every one a fluffy one) Tozer, Bonnie, Pam and Alan (PandA) Beard. And the crew on ground control at the Olau Line.

Annie Brickell of Bristol and her husband Garath. You sound a lovely lady and very happy. Good for you. Thanks for everything.

Heather Frisby asked about where to send her own tries at writing. I reckon magazines are a good way of getting started. Just send them in and hope. And keep on trying. Sounds like advice for something else.

Eileen Dover, whoever that might be, from Blyth in Northumberland. Liked the letter with jokes about a wooden leg. But try pulling the other one, it's got splinters on!

Tracie Field from New Zealand only sent in one joke but it was a really good one. Thanks a lot and if you keep on reading my adventures, you might even recognise it some time.

Pat and Mike Day, and their new daughter. Thanks for the letter and *everything*. That 'everything' should get the neighbours talking!

Sorry you didn't win a prize, Mrs Durham of Norwich, but thanks anyway.

And I hope Stephen Cooke of Cheltenham hasn't already spent the ten pound prize, because he hasn't got it. Nice try, though.

Loved the poem, Iris Gray of Orton Waterville. Shame you left out the frillies, but there it is.

I liked the shaggy Edgar joke, Lesley Barnes from Netherton, but I'm afraid I have a disappointment. As you'll see from this book, my Publisher has cut right down on the number of pages I'm allowed for dedications, and there just isn't going to be room for that great long list of people you wanted mentioning. So, Colin, Nigel, Helen, Simon, Mick, Colin, Yvette, Lynne, Susan, Clem, Gary, Carolyn, Tina, Ken, Bretton F.C., Peterborough F.C., Karen, John, Annette, Wayne, Angela, new baby, 1st Bretton Cubs, Scouts and Venturers. The bar staff of the Roundhead. Sorry I can't get in all the details about you all.

Janet Collins is still nursing. Thanks for the news, Janet. Keep it up. Well, you know what I mean.

Alastair Pirrie gets a mention in the ELO's hit 'Rockaria' so now he gets a mention in *Confessions Of A Gasman* as well, so isn't that nice for him. Actually Loony Linda asked for your name to be mentioned and she comes from Northallerton. So good luck to ALASTAIR PIRRIE.

Miss Lesley Dey from Aberdeen sent in a nice couple. I always like a lady with a nice couple. No frillies, though!

Ruth Logan has appeared in these columns before. She's still at Loughborough College of Technology and this time she sent in some lovely jokes. Thanks a lot.

Keith Bailey of Burnley sent in some amazing jokes, and even a picture. Liked it all, and sorry there was only the one prize.

And that's about all. Keep writing. Send in jokes and pictures and frillies. Specially the frillies. And rock on.

Chapter One

'Jonny?'

'Yes?'

'Are you having trouble with it?'

'Well . . .'

She walks over closer to me, her hips wiggling in a way that would bring Nelson down off his Column and has Edgar sitting up and begging. As my strides are not of the loosest, I wish that I could get hold of a bottle of lust-remover.

'Can't you get it out?'

'I think I can get it out, Tracey, but after it's out, I'm not sure I'll be able to get it in again.'

She leans over me, certain parts of her body digging into me and giving me the twice-over. Sad to say her armpits are not exactly her charmpits, but I can put up with a lot from a bird who looks like Tracey Tyttefiedler, and I'm not even going to give you a guess how she pronounces that.

'Perhaps if I reach down and give you a hand.'

'I think it's coming.'

'So soon?'

I smile modestly.

'I'd still like to get my fingers around it and give it a feel to make sure it's hard enough.'

She gets her fingers around it and gives it a firm squeeze,

like seeing if the bananas are ripe enough. She seems pleased with the ripeness of my banana.

'Very good, Jonny. That's lovely and firm. Do be careful and don't let it get too hard. There's a real problem of getting it in if it's too hard, remember?'

She's telling me.

(Publisher's Note: Sorry to appear so early, but I do have a responsibility to the shareholders. I hope Mister May is not going to let this go on for too long. It's all too clear what is going on with this lady, and our lawyers are beginning to sweat a bit.)

He's only jealous about me being able to make it go on for so long. And as for the shareholders, I reckon that they've probably been taken over by the Arabs. Still, if that happens, and you get into trouble, you can always turn the other sheikh.

After that bit of Eastern promise, back to Miss Tyttefiedler.

'If you get it too hard, then there's always a danger of something splitting.'

What a nasty thought. Most girls I know are really loyal and wouldn't split on anyone.

'Jonny. Do you know what to do if it has got too hard?'

'Maybe stretch the opening.'

'Possibly.'

Now she's so close that you couldn't even get a copy of the wit and wisdom of Nicholas Parsons between us.

'I think that I'd rather you used some kind of grease. Makes the connection so much easier.'

'I'm all in favour of that, Tracey.'

She gives one of those laughs that makes you wonder whether you're coming or going. I know what I'm doing, and I'll give you a subtle clue. I'm not going.

(Publisher's Note: Groan.)

That's twice in two pages, smartiepants. I'm the one who makes the jokes around here. I'm not saying that my Publisher is thick, but it's hard to believe that he's not born in Birmingham. I remember when we had that drought, and my Publisher suggested that the way to save water was to dilute it.

'I used to know a fellow that was always getting it too hard. He used to make it slip in nicely by putting a bit of spit on the end of his fingers and rubbing it on.'

These magic moments from Tracey's murky past are getting Edgar into dreadful straits, and I'm not talking about Dover. If she goes on like this any longer, rubbing it up and down and keeping it hard, then I won't answer for the consequences.

'Leave it for too long and it goes soft, and we know how much use that is, don't we, Jonny?'

By Swee and Knee!

'Right, Jonny. I think the time has come when you're going to have to really push it in. Don't be shy. Ram it in. Harder the better.'

'Shouldn't you take your hands off it first?'

Tracey gives another of her special laughs. The kind that would make even Lord Longford turn in his blue pencil.

'Yes. Suppose it might be easier. Now, off you go. Good. Excellent. In no time at all you'll be able to do that for housewives all over England.'

'Will they be grateful?'

'Most of them.'

Can't win them all, I suppose.

I'm pleased to say that I manage it first time, and the connection is safely . . . connected. Tracey is delighted. Actually, I find that I generally succeed in satisfying most ladies with whom I come. I mean come into contact.

'Now it's in, can you try and turn it round? See if you can get your hand in to do it.'

Well, I did say that Tracey is quite a well-built lady. So I try and she squeals, with pleasure.

'Lovely. I honestly think you're one of the very best I've

ever had. If you push it in a bit further you'll be able to get it stuck.'

'What happens if I do get it stuck?'

Fair question, you must admit.

'Then I take this hacksaw and I cut it off.'

Trouble is, Miss Tyttefiedler is not joking. What's more, I do get it stuck, and she is as good as her word. Her dainty fingers take up the saw and in a few quick strokes she has it off.

Nasty feeling to see something you've given a lot of affection to lying there on the floor, as much use as a rare steak at a vegetarian wedding. Quite sends chills up and down my Pennine Chain, it does.

Jonny must be joking, I hear you saying.

(Publisher's Note: If he is, then it's the first time that I've ever noticed it.)

I'm not going to say that my Publisher is one of the great gourmets of life. Not quite with your Fanny Cradocks, or your Delia Smiths or Robert Carriers – who must have made a lot of money having invented Carrier bags – but my Publisher is up there with the biggest. Offer him a night of wine, wild women and song and he'll ask you if he can see the label on the wine bottle first.

But as far as that goes, and the further the better, I am telling you the absolute truth. Every word in the above bit of conversation is true, right down to that horrible moment with the hacksaw. So how can this be? I hear you say. Is it the end of Edgar? Are the credentials never to be seen again?

My credentials are obscene but not hurt.

What of Jonny's testimonials? Is he really cut off in his prime?

Tell you this much: It's all to do with my new job. Those of you who checked the title of a book before reading it will already know. Those of you who don't might still think this is the *Critique of Purest Unreason* by Bertrand Muscle.

The new job is all right, so far. In case you still don't know what it is, here's a little inkling. And if you've never inkled, you haven't lived.

Like Jumping Jack Flash, this new job of yours truly is a gas, gas, gas.

Chapter Two

My Publisher once suggested that I go out and get a job working for the Ministry of Pensions and National Couldn't Care Less. Thought it would make a really funny book, is what he says. I tell him it'd be about as funny as going and telling a bunch of Manchester United fans they're all poofs.

Funny as a barbed wire jockstrap.

Anyway, welcome to Volume Nine of the amazing adventures of yours truly, Jonathan May. In a few pages my dear Publisher will come tiptoeing in with his size fourteen wellies to remind me to give a plug to the other eight books. Don't worry, I'll stall him as long as I can.

Before we go any further, I'd like to give you a quickie. Get you in the mood.

I don't know what for, but the bloke who tells it me says it'll get anyone in the mood for anything. Get 'em smiling and you're halfway there. Most girls actually laugh at me but that doesn't mean I'm nearly there.

Here's the quickie. Three men all lost in the desert. An Englishman, a Scotsman and a Brummie. They all meet up right in the middle of the Saraha.

The Englishman's carrying a big umbrella. The Scotsman's

got a rifle on his shoulder. The Brummie's sweating along with a car-door.

Brummie looks at the Englishman. 'What the blurry 'ell are you carryin' that for?'

'Well, old sport,' says the Englishman. 'I'm carrying this brollie so that if it rains it'll keep the jolly old rain orf me, and if it doesn't, then I shall use it as a jolly old parasol. What?'

'Oh, I see,' says the Brummie. Then, to the Scotsman: 'What the blurry 'ell are you carryin' that gun for?'

'Weel,' says the big yin. 'I'm carrying this wee gun so that I can shoot any game we might meet. Then we can drink its blood and eat the meat. Ye ken?'

'No, I ain't Ken. I'm Enoch,' says the Brummie, 'Enoch' being a good old Black Country name. Or a white country if Enoch prefers.

'I say,' says the Englishman. 'What about you? Why are you toting along that jolly old car door?'

His part will be played by Ian Carmichael if they ever make a film of this joke.

'I ain't blurry daft,' says Enoch. 'You and you'm blurry umbrellas and blurry guns.'

'But this is the middle of the Sahara Desert,' says Ian . . . I mean the Englishman. 'What use is that car door you're carrying?'

'Ar,' says Enoch, rubbing his nose in a meaningful manner. 'If it gets any blurry hotter I can roll the blurry window down.'

There you are, guys and gals of the J.M. fan club. A golden quickie for your collection. Each one privately printed and bound in its original covering. These jokes will surely increase in value over the years and become a wonderful investment. Produced in a limited edition, limited to only three hundred and forty-five thousand copies, you must order now at the special privilege price of only two hundred and eighty pounds.

Before I start gassing on and explain about how I get this

new job, there are a few loose ends to be tied up. I bet you like having your loose end tied up, Missus!

First off I have to thank all of you who've sent me letters and jokes and birthday cards (September 24th, folks) and specially those lovely ladies who've rummaged through their drawers and sent along their drawers. Uncle Angus and his knicker stall in West Bromwich depends on the constant flow of frillies, so keep them coming. All of you who've sent in any kind of contribution will find that they've got a mention at the front of either of this volume, or in a subsequent book.

While I'm on doing this bit, I suppose I might as well humour my Publisher, who has *no* sense of humour himself, and mention the other books that lots of you have bought, but there must still be a few of you somewhere that haven't actually bought *all* of them. All available from your local bookstall, or direct from Sphere Books. If you can't get any of them, then write to the people at Sphere. Play your cards right and you might even get a nice letter from my Publisher.

I must say he occasionally has a nice idea. He once crossed a potato with a bath sponge. Tastes horrible, but it mops up the gravy a treat.

Those wonderful people who've read all of my merry tales can go and make a cup of coffee or something while I tell the other poor misguided folk what they're missing. Never mind the cup of coffee, just go and do something for a page or so.

When I come down from Great Barr, which is just to the north of Birmingham, I get my first job at Stoppers of Knightsbridge, which is a classy store and where I am first introduced to the swinging London scene. And Edgar gets plenty of swinging.

This is all told in *Confessions Of A Shop Assistant.*

After my spectacular exit from there, I take myself in hand and get stuck into the travel business. It's a backs to the wall operation, specially when the owner, Rupert Colt, is anywhere around. *Confessions Of A Travel Courier* proves that Jonny

May will not bend over backwards for everyone.

An Academy for the daughters of gentlefolk sounds the type of establishment that Jonny would be able to take in his stride. Sadly, *Confessions Of A Games Master* shows that the truth is sometimes stranger than fiction.

Or *Ruth is no stranger to friction* as a notice said outside a new massage parlour in Moseley.

How many of you have spotted my deliberate mistake? Actually I forgot that I joined the Neapolitan Ice for a short time, but it tries hard to erase itself from my memory. Any resemblance between Constable Jonathan May and Jack Regan is purely ridiculous. But it's all in *Confessions From The Beat.*

What could be better than taking charge of a strip club in the heart of deepest Soho, and having lots of lovely ladies at your beck and call? Lots of things, friends.

And few of them were beck girls, but I fear that all of them were call girls.

Confessions From A Strip Club is not the happiest of my adventures.

What can I say about *Confessions Of A Housewife!?!?!?*

(Publisher's Note: Not too much, I hope. This is going on longer than a business lunch with Mister May. I have never seen a human being eat so much, so fast.)

And I have never seen a Publisher who pays so little so slowly.

I was talking about the time that I have to run a house for a few weeks, to do a favour for a lady who has been doing me several favours. Favour of the month, she was.

Confessions Of A Sex Clinic is the shortest on record. No, dear, I don't mean *that*. It's the shortest time that I hold down a job. Not to mention the time that I spend holding down the ladies who come to the Sex Clinic. They come along, and they come inside. Never seen so much coming since my last wife-swapping party in Great Barr. I know I don't have a wife to swap, but you don't need a cushion to play musical chairs.

Last time we met, I had been conned by my never-loving brother Morrie. Under threat of having my face turned into a lace curtain by Knuckles Newman, Morrie tricks me into being the active member – which is something I don't normally mind – in his firm. Read all about it, mates, in *Confessions Of A Stuntman.* Not a pretty tale, and it ends with yours very truly finding himself right in it.

I mean IT.

Spelled with a 'Sh' as in a certain brand of tonic water.

I know most of my jobs seem to finish with Jonny in the you know what, but 'Stuntman' really ends up like that, with me dropping into several thousand gallons of 'it' from a very great height.

But, as you would expect, I manage to come out of it smelling of . . . . . . Shhhhhhhhhh . . . . . . it!

And what of my dear brother Morrie?

I can only give you some idea if you've not yet met my brother by telling you about a competition that Morrie once runs in a magazine for swingers. First prize is a honeymoon for three.

Last I see of Morrie after I've landed in 'it' is a dirty pair of heels as he vanishes with my money. Then nothing for a couple of weeks, when I get a card from him.

Posted in Hong Kong. Says he's spending a lot of time playing ping pong. Taken up bell-ringing but keeps on getting the ring wrong. Joined some scouts out there around a camp-fire for a sing-song. And saw a good movie on local telly that he liked. Something about a big ape on the Empire State Building.

(Publisher's Note: Sounds rather like 'King Kong' to me.)

There he goes again. Leaping about on my jokes with his hob-nailed mouth. He's hardly the most subtle of men. My

Publisher's idea of subtle humour is to put a plastic dog turd under a whoopee cushion.

I'm glad that Morrie has left the country for a while. It means that I can walk along a street without having to keep looking over my shoulder to make sure he hasn't got a disastrous new idea for making money.

For himself.

I still remember the time he tried to cross a beaver with a kangaroo. He wanted to get a fur coat with pockets.

He's the gristle in the pork chop of life, is my brother.

Which makes Melanie the lipstick stain on the glass of life. Melanie is my sister, and I have also received another post-card from her.

'I have found a new man in my life.' Which makes a change from the life in some of her men. 'He is connected with a sort of finance firm and keeps making me.' I am not at all surprised. Oh, sorry, she goes on . . . 'Keeps making me offers I cannot refuse. If you or Morrie ever have any children, Don Boremeonle says he will be the Godfather to them. He keeps talking about the cosy roster, whatever that is. He says that if I am not a good girl he will fit me up with a new overcoat. Funny that as most men buy me clothes for when I *am* a good girl. All for now. The Don says he is going to take me for a ride. Melanie.'

It's posted in Miami, Florida, so if he has taken her 'for a ride' there is nothing I can do. Maybe he has just taken her for a ride. I'm not that worried, as I know my little sister well enough to be sure that she can look after herself. A circus owner tried to get her to wrestle naked with an alligator, but the alligator got scared.

That's my family dealt with, apart from my old mum and dad who are still living in Great Barr, in the same house. Last time I go there I am heart-broken to see they have finally pulled down the Beacon Cinema, where I had so many interesting experiences in my youth.

I'm in there once, snogging (remember snogging?) away in the stalls when there's a lot of shouting down the front. Bloke yelling his head off.

Everyone tells him to shut up, and there's a bit of a hush for a couple of minutes, then he starts off yelling again. Making a fantastic noise so you can't hear whether the Monster or the Ape is winning. Down comes the Manager after a session with the fish and chips in his office, and tells the fellow to keep quiet or get out.

Still the noise goes on, like a great Discorde flying right over your head.

'Right. I'm calling the police,' says the Manager, striding back up the aisle to the accompaniment of cheers and lighted matches.

By now everyone's more interested in the bloke yelling out than they are in the film, and the fuzz arrives to whistling noises and a badly-aimed carton of orange juice. Actually, it isn't empty. It is empty of orange juice, but not empty.

Not very nice people in Great Barr in those days. A lot better than some of the patrons of the old Queen's Cinema in West Bromwich, but that's another horror story.

'Do you mind keeping a bit of hush, sir?' says the local law.

'Aaarggggghhhhrrrrhhhgggaaaaaarrggh,' says the man in the middle of the stalls. Very loud. Like he's trying to drown out 'Crossroads' on next door's telly. And what a good idea that would be.

'If you don't keep quiet, then I shall have to ask you to accompany me to the nearest police station, where it is not beyond the bounds of possibility that you may fall down a flight of stairs and then try and damage police property with your head.'

'Yaaeargh,' replies the bloke.

'Very well, sir. You leave me no option. Can I have your name and address?'

'Uarrrrrrrrrr.'

'Come on, sir. You're spoiling the enjoyment of everyone. Just tell me where you've come from.'

'From . . . Ooooooohhhhh . . . from the . . . Aaaaarghhh . . . from the balcony.'

That sort of thing was always happening at the Beacon Cinema. Still, it's a shame it's gone. Any of you who happen to be driving from Walsall to Birmingham or from West Bromwich to Sutton, or anyone going through that big junction at the Scott Arms, go past the site where it used to be. It's a fantastically busy junction now, but I can remember when it was so quiet that the traffic lights only changed once a day.

Still, my old mum and dad are quite happy up there, though mum's cooking hasn't got any better. And there's no way it could get worse. She still thinks that the only way to crack an egg is with a tin-opener.

Anyway, that brings you up to date where everyone is and what they're doing, which in the case of most of the members of the May family is as little as possible.

I am faced with two choices.

Get another job as soon as possible.

Or go and sign on.

Those of you who have read one or two of my earlier adventures will know by now that all is not light and warmth between the folk at the Labour and yours very truly. We get on about as well as Johnny Speight and Mary Whitehouse.

Last time I have to go in there, I find that there is a great long queue all waiting while the staff finish off a vital and important piece of business. I'll give you a clue what it is. Something to do with Typhoo. That's it. You've got it to a 't'. Or a 'tea'.

So it's going to be back to work. Straighten my shoulders. Chin up. Stomach in. Nose to the grindstone. Best foot forwards. Finish up looking like the Hunchback of Notre Dame. Very appealing he was. Name rang a bell. Ran around like the clappers. One of the bells of the ball.

I glance through the Sits Vac column of the paper, but nothing catches my eye. I need something that'll give me a challenge.

More important I need something that'll give me some money. After the farce of the stuntman, I have a few of the crisp oncers left, but they won't last long. I'm still living rent-free in the flat of the lovely Liz James, who regulars will know is the true love of my life, but who goes off all over the world more often than I've had hot jobs. At the moment she's somewhere sur le Continent and I haven't heard from her for ages.

The Notting Hill place is fine, as it gives me a base to operate from, and even better, it doesn't cost me anything. But I have to eat, and tins of soup and loaves of bread and eggs don't come cheap. Chickens come cheep, but the rest don't.

I am so hard up that I actually consider pawning some of my records. But Doctor Hook and John Stewart and Dylan and the Eagles and New Riders are to be saved. For a post-card comes fluttering though the letterbox bringing news of relief.

It is the greatest relief since my old man ate a whole box of Exlax by mistake. Felt as if the world had dropped out of his bottom.

The postcard is a hand-tinted photo of some cruddy beach in France. Hand-tinted by some colour-blind person with a strong stomach. Makes the sea look the colour of one of my mum's mutton stews.

Bright green!

Despite that, it is more welcome than a new opening batsman for England.

'Will be at Liverpool Street Station on Thursday at three. Missing you and look forward to making up for lost time. Lots of love, Liz.'

Smashing!

Quickie to get you over the suspense of turning the page into the next chapter.

What goes 'Woof, tick, woof, tick?'

A watch-dog.

Chapter Three

Visiting Liverpool Street Station reminds me of the time that my Uncle Angus used to work on the railways. Now he's an exporter.

Get it?

(Publisher's Note: No.)

I'm not saying that my Publisher isn't very bright, but I would whisper to you that he is a loyal supporter of a certain football club whose name begins with 'C' and ends with 'A'. And the middle letters are 'HELSE'. I must admit that they need all the support they can get. But I reckon the only kind of support that would do them much good would be a solid gold jockstrap.

Uncle A's an exporter.

Ex-porter. Now do you get it?

Forget it.

I haven't been to this particular station before, and find it's not much like on the Monopoly Board at home. Despite Uncle Nick coming and spilling the contents of his inch-thick parsley sauce butties over the board, it's still a whole lot cleaner than the real thing.

I'm not one to give you a wrong impression, but I must say that I have never seen a station where the pigeons went around in wellies and the toilets are out of order more often than a drunk politician.

The platform is a bit cluttered with a handful of jolly men who have been drinking a bit too much of Chateau Meths '77. There are several porters standing around with the cheerful faces that I associate with a wet Sunday in Llandudno.

'Can you tell me what time the train gets in from Harwich?' I ask the nearest one. I know the card says three, but I believe British Rail's timetables like I believe in Father Christmas.

'Dunno.'

I jingle a handful of tap washers in my pocket with a meaningful smile and he snaps to attention. 'What time?' I ask again.

'Three o'clock, sir. Over there. Do you want a porter, sir?'

'Thank you. I suppose you'd like me to give you a tip, wouldn't you?'

'Up to you, sir. But I reckon it'd be welcome.'

'Of course. As a reward for your charming and helpful attitude, I shall give you a tip.'

His hand shoots out quick as a policeman's notebook, and I smile once more at him.

'My tip is never to try and catch a train departing at twelve-fifty.'

'What? What do you mean?'

'Because it's ten to one that you'll miss it.'

The train comes in only eleven minutes late, which I guess British Rail think is as good as half an hour early. Out pour the usual crowd of Scandinavian students. All rucksacks, good teeth, rimless glasses and blonde hair. Peering around them like they've just stepped off a spaceship on a strange planet.

I don't see Liz James at first, and my heart sinks lower than a penguin's pooper. My prospects have never been smaller and if she doesn't come home today, then I fear I shall have to make that dreaded trip to the friendly neighbourhood pawnbroker. May his balls tarnish.

There is a great crush of foreign tourists swirling around me. A sea of little Dutch caps envelopes me, and then the Rotterdam Hollanders move on. The next Common Market crew are from Belgium. I can tell that as they are all eating chips and spitting all over the place. Did you know that the Belgians are the only people in the world who have to have their windscreen wipers on the *inside* of the window?

They all seem as they are going to go camping. Silly ruckers!

Suddenly, among the chattering mob I feel a hand delving around the jewel casket. The only person who plays pocket billiards on my table is Jonathan May and I reach down, ready to give this naughty person a piece of . . . well, whatever she wants.

Providing it is a she!

I've heard about these gay tourists coming over here. The British backs to the wall attitude isn't just because we're slowly going bankrupt.

It is a she. There are so many people pushing us towards the ticket barrier that I can't see who it is, but the hand that I grab that is grabbing me is too small to be a fellow. Whoever she is, the lady is having herself a ball.

Or even two.

I'm through the barrier, and the hand is still there. Still hanging on to what it's got. And babe I'm sure that it's got a lot.

At last I can look around and see who this imp of mischief is, clutching me by the short and curlies.

Yes, I know I know who it is.

And it is.

'Hello, Jonny.'

'Hello, Liz.'

'Long time no see.'

'As the stale fish finger said.'

'God, you haven't changed.'

'Are you sorry?'

'No, Jonny. I'm not sorry. I've always liked you the way you are.'

We kiss.

She is looking terrific. Actually, it has been quite a long time since Edgar went off on the long and winding road to the passion pit, so any lady with roughly the right equipment in roughly the right places would be welcome. But Liz really is something a bit special.

She's very sun-tanned and her hair is bleached a couple of shades lighter. Her shades are actually darker, with golden rims. She's wearing a light grey t-shirt, with the words 'Virginia Is For Lovers' on it. Either she has bought it a size too small, or the French food has done her a lot of good and made her twice the attraction she was. That's an exaggeration, but Liz certainly seems to be busting out all over. As usual she is not wearing a bra. The crowd is thinning out and we are able to walk two abreast.

I know I haven't *said* she's let go of the heirlooms, but of course she has. Liz isn't the sort of girl to insist on making a pubic exhibition of herself.

'How about another kiss, then Jonny?'

Before you can say 'Xanadu' – and that's for fans of Dave Dee, Thingie, Nosey, Whatsit and Titch – her arms are round me and she's pulling me past the bookstall to a quiet corner near some phone booths.

I know that many of you ladies are interested in fashion notes, so I'll complete Liz's wardrobe. Below the t-shirt there is a fascinating area of bare midriff, and then the top of her jeans. Tucked into a hand-tooled pair of brown cowboy boots.

I love a bit of hand-tooling, myself, don't you, missus?

If she sucks any harder my tongue's going to vanish right the way down her deep throat. Maybe she never had any breakfast as my lips are getting a good nibbling. I find that I have both hands full. One with the top and the other with the bottom.

'Have you got a bunch of keys in your pocket, Jonny, or are you just pleased to see me?'

Edgar is making his presence felt. Liz regards him as her present, so she also gets her present felt.

'Jonny, it's no good but I'll have to . . . '

'The Gents' is over there past the eaterie, but I don't know where the . . . '

'Not that, twit. You know what I mean!'

She shows me what she means by unzipping the strides faster than Lionel Blair criticising someone else's dress sense.

'Not here,' I squeak, my voice sounding like I've just failed in the barbed wire high hurdles.

'That phone box.'

She's a jolly joker, is Liz James. Imagine suggesting that we go into a tiny, glass telephone box, right in the middle of Liverpoool Street Station and do thingie!

What a silly idea.

Even if I was to be dragged there by my mutton chopper, I still wouldn't . . .

'Ouch.'

She has and I would.

And we do.

'You look a bit pale, Jonny. Have you been holding your own?'

'I haven't had anyone else to hold it for me, Liz,' I say, with a note of pathos.

'Wasn't Pathos one of the Three Musketeers?'

'Come on in where it's nice and warm.'

I know just where she means.

Actually, a telephone box isn't the most comfortable place in the world for doing what we are doing. But Liz still has a firm grip on my most precious possession, and is giving it more little tugs that the *QE2*. The door shuts on us, and there we are.

Face to face.

Eye to eye.

Toe to toe.

Nose to nose.

Finding how easy it is to stomach each other.

And that is not all.

'Can you get it out?'

'It is out.'

'I don't mean that, love. I mean this.'

I wish sometimes that ladies didn't wear such tight jeans. Anyway, I am not going to risk illegal entry through the zip. A lad can come to a nasty end like that, and I have the scars to prove it. It's worse than trying to change into swimming trunks under a pocket hankie on a crowded beach. But eventually we get them dropped to a convenient level around the hips. Liz is wearing a tiny pair of . . . wait for it Elias Banglestein . . . here it comes . . . knickers ! ! ! !

Very pale blue, and all silky. Tight round the waist and even tighter round the happy valley. I manage to slip in a dextrous digit.

'Oh, that's lovely.'

She's massaging Edgar like he's just been pulled unconscious out of the canal. Normally I'd expect her to get going on the kiss of life, but there's hardly room to stand in the phone box, and you can't always have it on a plate. Incidentally, I notice that the number of the phone is 6969X. That's the sort of number I love to roll my tongue around.

I bend down and Liz straightens up, and then we both sort of melt into each other, like a hot knife sliding through a block of chocolate mousse. Incidentally, don't forget that chocolate mousse can be tricky stuff to handle. Let it slip off the plate and: Hoots mon, you'll have mousse loose aboot your hoose!

We are moving on well together, like she's never been away,

when I feel a nasty draught round the Khyber Pass, and there's a stabbing pain in the middle of my back.

'Are you two young people making a telephone call or making love?' says this upper-class woman's voice. Have you ever noticed that nearly all upper-class twits have that sort of voice? Like they've got both legs through one leg of their Y-fronts. I reckon it's all that bouncing around in the saddle when they go hunting. Like they've got a sharp stick up their jacksies.

'Sorry,' says Liz, not wanting to answer the sarcastic old bag with an honest reply.

'Well, I'm waiting to come.'

'So am I,' I say, noticing that the windows of the call-box are getting nicely steamed up.

'Well be quick, young man.'

'I'm doing my best, aren't I, Liz?'

'Yes, love,' says the lovely Miss James, using her inside muscles to do lovely things to my outside muscle.

'Shut the door, will you, madam. We're getting a nice fug in here.'

Now I knew that's how you spell it, but it isn't how you pronounce it. Not for the benefit of this rude dowager, who gasps like she's caught the butler at the best sherry and goes out of our snug little box.

Edgar is enjoying Liz's snug little box, and leaping about all over the place, like a frisky young colt. Not a Colt 45, even in centimetres.

Round about thirty, if you must know.

(Publisher's Note: Thirty centimetres! Don't believe it. That's more than a foot.)

I'm not talking about the length of my feet!

(Publisher's Note: I know that. But I just don't believe it. Nobody is that well endowed.)

Last time he gets his wife to touch him up in bed she just

giggles and tells him to put it under the pillow so she can smoke it later.

I don't want to give you the impression that my Publisher is not very athletically enthusiastic in the matters of a bit of thingie. However, and by the by, it's not so long since he comes up to me after he's just asked me to write him another of my adventures, and says he wants some help.

'What's wrong?'

'I seem to have a bit of a job . . . you know . . . sort of . . . raising it.'

I raise an eyebrow. 'Raising it?'

'Raising *it*!'

I raise a smile. 'I can help. Morrie has a friend who's a sort of chemist.'

Like Crippen got a sort of a divorce. Actually this mate of Morrie specialises in what the blue-boys call 'certain substances'. But he does a bit on the side for ladies. And what lady isn't interested in having a bit on the side?

So I get hold of a special pill from him.

'Make a bit of limp celery like an iron girder,' he says. 'Very quick acting.'

Like a bit part in 'Crossroads'.

I give it to my Publisher next time he takes me for a business lunch. We get some funny looks from the other dossers at the soup stall down by the Thames, but it never worries my Publisher. Last of the great misers, he is.

'You're sure it'll work?' he asks.

'Sure. It'll act instantly. Or maybe even a bit quicker than that.'

'I'll try it tonight,' he says.

Off he goes, forgetting to pay for the tea and bread and butter, as usual, and I see him again the very next day at his office. Four walls held apart by eight foot of threadbare carpet.

'How did it go? The pill? Work all right did it?'

He groans.

'What went wrong?'

'I'm not very good at swallowing pills,' he says.

'So?'

'So I swallowed it slowly, and all it did was give me a stiff neck.'

Shouldn't really have torn you away there as Liz and I are nearing a very interesting stage in our passionate affair in the phone box at Liverpool Street Station. I find that the long lay-off has slowed down my speeding-up. I mean speeded up my slowing-down. Either way, I'm in danger of . . . how shall I put it? I didn't say 'where' I said 'how'. In danger of eating my pudding before anyone else has finished their main course.

I glance round the box for a way of slowing down. There's always the graffiti. 'I would like to look up Marianne Faithfull's knickers.' Wouldn't we all?

That doesn't slow me down at all. In fact the thought of one of my most favourite lovely ladies simply speeds me up a bit.

'A.C. loves C.W.' I like Country and Western myself, as it happens. Waylon Jennings and Willy Nelson and Don Williams and big John R. Cash.

'Here I stand, broken-hearted. Paid ten pence and never started.'

I know a different version of that.

There's a rapping on the glass like a demented woodpecker. Although things are approaching their hypotenuse, or do I mean apex? Anyway, things are just about to happen but I manage to wriggle my head round on my shoulders, and there is the same old lady with her face pressed flat against the window just behind me. I can't imagine what she thinks must be going on, but her mouth is open wider than a drowning goldfish.

'Will you be long?' she mouths through the glass.

'No.' I shake my head to emphasise what I'm saying, and to try and distract attention from what I'm doing.

'Come on, Jonny,' moans Liz, kissing me very gently all

over the face like an erotic butterfly.

'Come on, young man!'

It's true what they say. You can't hope to satisfy two women at the same time.

'I'm coming,' I whispered to my love.

'I'm going,' I call to the miserable old lady outside the phone box.

It's like getting a crossed line. I love that, actually. Never hang up until I've had a good earhole. Shocking, isn't it? But I bet you do it as well. Once heard someone talking about booking a field for a parachute jump. Honest! I know that's not very funny, but it is a bit peculiar and it is true.

The earth moves beneath our feet, and we both clutch and moan a lot, rather like a couple of wrestlers on telly. Aware that the old lady is not alone, and that there is a healthy queue taking an unhealthy interest in our activity, I carefully ease Edgar from the tunnel of love, and tuck it back into the strides as quick as I can, narrowly avoiding a nasty bit of decapitation in the zip. Covered by me, Liz wriggles back into her knickers, pulling her jeans over her lovely little bottom.

Some birds have bottoms like a couple of sacks filled with cold porridge, and that always puts me off my oats. But Liz has a tight little bum, more like a couple of bread rolls, baked to perfection. You can tell they're perfection by giving them a squeeze.

The buns, not the bum.

Oh, I don't know.

'That was great, love. Really nice to be back.'

'Thanks for having me.'

She grins in a way that sets Edgar stirring stickily in the purple passion-huggers. 'Thank you for coming.'

She's only got a small hold-all, and you know what they say about the size of a bird's bag! Like the size of a bloke's hooter. Jonny, in case you are wondering, has a conk that is not renowned for its smallness.

We pick up the bag and walk out of the phone box to meet the other bag, who is hopping up and down like Rodney Marsh when someone comes between him and the cameras.

'You've finished at last. I hope you enjoyed it, both of you!'

'Yes thanks.'

'I cannot understand why it took you so long.'

'Sometimes the connection takes a bit of time.'

The one thing that unites people is hatred of the Post Office, and who can blame them. Fewer users for their high-priced calls and letters. So what do you do? Put up the charges so that fewer still people use them so you put the charges up so fewer still people use them and then you put the charges up so that even . . .

(Publisher's Note: Mister May wanted us to carry on this sentence for three and a half pages, but I feel that you get the picture.)

Yes, we see.

The old lady stares at us, and I believe I detect the faint trace of a smile crossing her wrinkled features.

'They are too dreadful, the telephone people, aren't they?' she says.

There you are. We're already united against the Post Office and she's quite forgotten how long we kept her waiting while having it away.

'Yes,' says Liz, smiling sweetly. 'I wasn't sure we'd get through at all.'

'Tut, tut,' goes the crowd, all sympathetic to our nasty plight.

'Engaged?' asks the old lady, now beaming away like she's just evicted an elderly cripple from her basement flat.

'No,' says Liz. 'Not engaged. We're just good friends.'

Collapse of stout party.

Chapter Four

Thinking about bad tempered old ladies reminds me of the time that Uncle Angus, may his sporran never wither, goes into a chemist's shop in Birmingham. And this isn't the one where he goes into the chemist and says he wants a packet of shooting-brakes and they say: 'We haven't got any. Have you tried Boots?' And he replies: 'Yes, but it all ran out through the lace holes.'

No. It's not that joke.

Uncle Angus goes into the chemist's shop in Birmingham intending to get a packet of shooting-brakes.

I *know* it sounds like that joke, but it *isn't.* Just play hospitals and be patient.

When he walks into the shop it's empty, apart from the very grim-eyed, middle-aged lady assistant. Dressed in a white coat she looks like a cross between 'Doctor No' and Dracula's mother-in-law.

'Pardon me,' says Uncle Angus, knuckling his forelock at her, which is not to be tried if the fuzz are around. So don't any of you go knuckling your forelocks at anyone.

'What?' snaps the lady, face frozen solider than a Bird's Eye warehouse.

'I wonder if you could be of assistance?'

'I'm not standing stood here for my health.'

Manners might maketh man but they do damn-all for some women.

Uncle Angus wonders whether to ask for what he really wants or whether to chicken out and ask for a bottle of Lucozade. But his need is great so he takes a rain-check on the Lucozade.

'I wonder if you could serve me to six contraceptives, please, Miss?'

She bridles, which is on account of her horse-face. 'Don't you "Miss" me!'

'All right,' says Uncle Angus, game for anything. 'Better make it seven then.'

I am starting the day with a continental breakfast. A roll in bed with honey. And Liz James is a real honey, believe me.

The flat in Notting Hill is quite a nice one, but I realise now how lonely it has been without any feminine company. As regular readers will know there have been one or two ladies who have been willing to roll over and die for Jonny in the last few months, but the less said about that the better as Liz is sometimes rather jealous. And I have no desire at all to be cut off in my prime.

'Jonny?'

'Yes, love.'

'I've been thinking.'

The danger signal begins to flash in a small room at the back of my mind. When any lady starts looking at you in a pensive manner and tells you she's been thinking, then that's the time to run for the hills.

'What about?'

'You.'

'Me?'

'You.'

'Why me?'

'Because.'

It crosses my mind that a swift right cross to the jaw might snap her out of this. But it would also snap me out of a very nice rent-free apartment, *and* one of the nicest birds with whom I've ever had the pleasure.

So I hold my peace.

As it's early morning and I'm bursting for a Robert E. I also hold my piece.

'You've not had much luck with jobs since I've been away, have you?'

Oh, oh. The alarm bell is ringing loud enough to waken a night-shift worker at . . .

(Publisher's Note: The firm that Mister May mentions here is in enough trouble without them all coming out on strike about his so-called joke. Anyway, I'm waiting for delivery of one of their new models myself. Not that it affects my open-minded attitude.)

His mind isn't open. It's ruddy vacant.

'Well, I'm always unlucky with work.'

Liz laughs, which makes the mobile milk-shop even more mobile. The subject of her chat depresses me. It's rotten to be stuck inside a bedroom with the mobile blues again.

That seemingly meaningless sentence will only be understood by followers of Bob Dylan. When I mention my favourite sounds, I should say that I never bother to talk about Dylan or Elvis or the Everlys or Buddy Holly. But they're up there in the All-Time greats.

'Jonny. You make everything into a joke.'

'Not everything.'

'Yes, you do.'

'No. I don't make racialist jokes.'

'What about the Brummie jokes?'

Thinking she's scored a point, Liz pokes me with the point of her finger. Where she pokes me is a rather sore point of mine.

'I'm a Brummie. So I can make jokes about where I come from.'

I mean, my Uncle Nick is a typical Brummie. I remember the time that Aunt Rose tells him that he really ought to put on a clean pair of socks every day.

'Blurry good idea, our kid,' he says, grinning through a haze of roll-up and Guinness.

So he does like she says.

By the end of the week he can't even get his wellies on.

I won't bore you with the long conversation that Liz and I have in bed. It goes on for about two hours, but I admit that there are a couple of interruptions for which I could be charged with assault with a friendly weapon. It's impossible to have a serious talk with a naked bird. It takes such a short time to get down to the bare essentials.

What Liz is trying to tell me is that she reckons I ought to go out and get a job. Work. Labour. Strive.

And other words guaranteed to bring a dose of the wobblies to any decent Briton. I come over a little queer at the thought, and I won't make my usual joke about the little queer not liking it very much.

She does a lot of freelance work, herself. I'm never quite sure what it involves, but there seems to be a bit of escorting. And she's never short of money. I think it's better if I draw a veil over that side of Miss James. Or even seven veils.

Like that Salami wore.

I promise that I'll give the Sits Vac pages another going-over. Not that I have high hopes. Long ones, Yes. But high ones, No. I just can't face the prospect of sitting all day in a boring old office surrounded by sniggering girls who slump around, with their skirts round their waists, feet on the desks, their little blouses tight across their...

On the other hand...

But there isn't anything. Not even the prospect of eyeing

up copy-typists' knickers all day tempts me. My old man used to tell me to specialise. 'Always be a job for a specialist!' was his cry, spluttered out through a mouthful of old and mild. And you can spray that again.

A specialist. It's all very well for my old man saying that, but he never does much with being a specialist. Then again, there isn't a lot of call nowadays for wick trimmers on street lamps.

Liz is out all day, and when she comes back I am surrounded by papers and sunk into a deep depression just north of Notting Hill.

'Any interviews?'

'Oh, yes,' I riposte merrily. 'Russell and Michael and Eamonn and David. I hear Dick Cavett's jetting across from New York to talk to me.'

'Jonny?'

'Yes?'

Here we go again.

'I shall not bandy words with you.'

'Well, you shouldn't spend so much time riding horses!'

'But I like you very much. I want you around most of the time more than anyone else I have ever known.'

By Reg, Is and Tree! And by Off and Ice! This sort of talk can lead a chap to the altar before you can say 'Lovonorobey.'

I am not getting any younger – in fact the life that I lead sometimes amazes me in that I'm still alive. And I suppose that the odd thought about marriage has crossed my mind with silver. Further still along that road, I have to admit that Liz James is the girl with whom I'm most likely to.

But not yet.

Maybe in about another ten or fifteen years. I don't think she's really ready for matrimony either.

'And I love you, too, Liz. You know that I do. But I just don't seem to get on with work.'

This is ruining my supper. Lovely fluffy omelette. Spoiled

by the talk about employment. Go to egg on work. Or whatever it is.

'Tell you what.'

'What?'

'Tonight, we'll watch telly. Stick to ITV for a change. How about that?'

'ITV for a change! A change is as bad as nothing.'

'You watch "The Sweeney". That's on that channel.'

'That's the exception.'

'You always talk about "Crossroads".'

'I always talk about Birmingham, but that doesn't mean I'd like to live there.'

'Your Aunt Rose watches it all the time.'

'And when my Aunt Rose comes visiting she leaves her broomstick up the side entry. Why on earth should we condemn ourselves to that? What have we done to deserve it?'

'Nothing.'

'Nothing?'

'Nothing. You've done nothing about getting another job, so this can be your punishment. We'll watch it together. Not the programmes. Just the commercials.'

I breathe a heavy sigh of relief. I enjoy it so much that I try some more on for sighs.

'Why?'

'To give you an idea of the sort of job you'd like. It'll give us a start.'

'We'll lie in front of the fire and sip Southern Comfort, that wonderful drink that warms and thrills the mind and body and which I really reckon it's about time that the people who bring Southern Comfort to Britain send along a couple of cases of.'

'And try and think about a job.'

'Can we take off some clothes to try and relax? It'll help the start.'

Liz sniffs and walks away towards the bedroom. 'There won't be any more of that sort of thing, Jonny, until you buck up your ideas and find work. So tonight is the end of the beginning for you.'

'No more thingie? That sounds more like the beginning of the end. Or even the end of the end.'

I am sunk in desolation.

I'm blowed if she'll dictate to me how I spend my own evening. Just with her threats of keeping me off thingie. I shall be master in . . .

. . . her own flat.

'I'll turn the telly on, Liz.'

Actually her idea turns out to be quite a good one. The commercials give me lots of ideas.

But they are not ideas for jobs. More ideas for thingie.

Unless you call it a job spraying that tick on the bird's back for her to go and get all sweaty. Or unwrapping those chocolate bars that sexy chicks munch on when they're all alone and miles from anywhere. Apart for the film crew and three hundred spectators.

Then there's the job helping out with the ladies' frillies. And tights. And getting on lipstick. I suppose someone's got to take it off.

I have to say that I don't fancy prancing around in balloons and boats and all that. Nor do I honestly reckon it as the most beautiful drink in the world. I prefer 'Vimto', if the truth is to be told. Or Tizer, the Appetizer. I like something with a real bit of fizz.

'It's no good, Liz.' The ads are mainly incredibly boring and stupid. One or two are quite funny, like the metal men who fall about laughing at the humans with their old-fashioned potato. Despite their clever ad, I still reckon that all instant mash tastes amazingly like the real thing. The real thing being processed and pulped cardboard. Give me a real spud any day.

'There must be something that gets you really charged up and ready for anything.'

'There is.'

The one with Twiggy in it for a start.

We are lying on the furry rug with eyes glazed after four and a half hours of processed telly. It's like being hit over the head with eight hundredweight of noisy pink cotton-wool, and I'm not sure how much more I can stand. If the Russians ever get to hear about it they'll improve their brain-washing techniques a hundred per cent. No normal human being could stand such fearful punishment.

I've managed to keep sane by closing my eyes to the boring bits in between the commercials. Liz has fallen asleep twice, and I have passed a little time watching her. I get a real kick out of looking at a bird I fancy when she's kipping. Liz isn't over-dressed as bedtime is approaching. She's got a man's t-shirt on, with a beautiful silk-screen design on it and the words 'San Francisco'. The design includes two red hearts. One over the right C-cup filler and the other over the other.

If you're waiting to know what else the lovely lady is wearing, then you can go and sling your hook.

Nothing.

Which does a lot for her comfort and even more for old Edgar. The one-round engagement in the phone box has just whetted his appetite. And wetted the front of my strides, but that's a different story.

(Publisher's Note: And not a very pleasant one, if I may say so.)

He's so mean, that man. He goes to this fifty pence knocking shop off Curzon Street in Mayfair. Fifty pence! A few days after his visit he finds that he's got lots of uninvited guests around the very short and not too curlies. So he goes rushing back to the hole-sale emporium and complains to the lady who runs it.

'I've caught crabs in your place,' he screams.

'Don't you mean in your place?' she replies.

'It's not funny. I tell you I've caught crabs.'

'Well. What do you expect for only fifty pence? Lobsters?'

I make a couple of tries to get through the barrier, but she just crosses her legs and breaks my glasses. No. Not really, but she does make it clear that I'm not welcome below the waist until I get a job. I'm not saying that she gets chilly with me, but if they ever make a film of 'Eskimo Nell', they know where to look for the lead.

'Please.'

'No, Jonny, no Jonny. No, no, no.'

'Go on.'

'No, Jonny, no, Jonny be good.'

By Chuck and Berry! I don't need any long distance information to get the message.

'I mean it. Promise me you'll get a job, and then we'll get to it.'

The idea of polishing my backside on the top sheet with Liz is too much. It even over-rides my dislike of that other four-letter word. 'W.O.R.K.'

'All right.'

'Promise?'

'Yes.'

'Break that promise, and it's not the only thing of yours that'll be broken.'

'I'll start in the morning.'

'How?'

'Never mind the Indian impersonations, just believe me, Liz.'

'You'll start ringing round in the morning?'

'I'll ring around the roses, if that's what you want, my lovely lady.'

'Flattery gets you everywhere with me, Jonny, as you know.'

I hope so.

Actually, mentioning calling round reminds me of what to do if you want to burn a Brummie's ear.

Ring him up when he's doing the ironing.

Only problem is with ringing up about a job, I still haven't seen anything on the telly that approximates to the sort of employment that I could live with. I don't want to ride up and down hills on a bike peddling loaves of bread.

Or sit in a pub singing old-time songs with the letter 'E' in it.

Or help out selling soap powder by lisping 'Thpringy thoft.' That's thtupid.

Or join that crowd of loonies who go around flashing badges at each other to prove they've all got some kind of shabby habit by all joining the same Building Society. I always reckon they're a bit sinister. If you don't happen to have their little badge on then they all turn on you and tear you to pieces, like some science fiction movie.

I remember a brilliant Benny Hill sketch where he's an old woman who watches telly and thinks that the commercials are real. After a night of watching them, I know what he means.

'Tell me what you're going to try for, Jonny,' says Liz, sitting cross-legged on the pouffe, her t-shirt not even covering her exit never mind her entrance.

'Shhhhh. I want to watch all the way to the end. I've got one or two ideas.'

I am stalling, I am stalling, far away, as you can see. I am lying, I am lying, watching dark clouds nearing me.

It's not only Super-Rod who can do it.

I glance at my watch, trying not to notice that Liz has got off the pouffe – poor little pouffe – and is now lying half on and half off the sofa. From where I am it looks like an aerial view of the Cheddar Gorge.

And I do mean that she's gorgeous.

It is gone twelve.
think we ought to go up and get started.'

'Time for bed, Jonny. As you've given me your word, I

'Started?'

'There's a long night ahead.'

That's what Queen Guinevere said when she first saw Sir Boldasbras the Tall sitting at the Round Table.

(Publisher's Note: At last I've understood one of Mister May's jokes. It's a pun on the word 'night'. A long 'knight' is what he means. Rather good, that one. Well done. Jolly fine. Carry on.)

I don't know why I bother. I could be a brain surgeon, or out cleaning the sewers. It's the romance of those long wellies that gets me. You will spot from that Jonny May is a fan of the Perishers.

But my Publisher is amazing. He's the original Six Million Dollar Idiot.

He once comes up to me and tells me that he's having a lot of trouble getting it in. You know, 'it'. 'In.' Right.

'You're having trouble getting it in?' I reply, with that quick wit that has made me the scourge of Great Barr. I make Bruce Forsyth look like Max Bygraves.

'Yes. I just can't seem to manage to get it in at all these days.'

'Have you tried Vaseline?' I ask him.

'Why?' he says. 'Will that make it hard?'

Hang on. There's a commercial coming on right now that looks interesting. There's this good-looking fellow wearing overalls going up a front path. Knocking on the doors. Hand on the . . .

KNOCKERS!!!

I have never seen anything like them. They make Dolly Parton look like Twiggy. If she turns round quickly she'll sweep everything off the mantelpiece. *And* she's standing in the hall at the time.

She's got long black hair, hanging down to her . . . and even a bit below it. Through it I can glimpse a low-cut bra. Also black, with red ribbons. To contain those melons it must be a triumph of engineering that makes Concorde look ridiculous. Personally, I reckon that Concorde is already ridiculous, but you know what I mean.

'Good morning, Madam,' says the bloke at her door, looking at a bit of paper on a clipboard. He must be barmy. How can he keep his mind on his job, whatever that is?

The camera eases back and I can see more of the charms. Which is good luck for me, so I reckon they must be good luck charms.

I see now that she is wearing a transparent housecoat, as clear as spun glass, which reveals a great deal of her interesting bone structure. Ladies who wear glass housecoats shouldn't show bones. It's bad for my blood pressure. Edgar is amazed at what he is seeing. I can't wait to find out what it's going to be an advert for.

The camera pulls further back. It seems a bit shaky, and I wonder if it's hand-cranked. Liz has noticed my rising interest and is doing a good job of hand-cranking on me.

Below the waist this housewife is attractively garbed in black suspender belt. Black fishnet stockings. Lacy black knickers. And black patent-leather high-heel shoes.

Workaday clothes for the average lady of the land to answer the door in.

What can it be an ad for?

'I've come to convert you, Madam,' says the bloke in the overalls.

So that's it! By Watch and Tower! These Jehovah's Witnesses have changed their approach since I last closed my door on one of them. This is very down-market. I've heard of taking religion to the people but this is ridiculous.

'Of course. Come right on in and have a look at what I've got.'

He doesn't have to go in to see what she's got. Anyone could see it at a half mile range. If they happened to be passing by and fell off their ladder and broke their binoculars!

'What's this?'

'You know very well what that is, Liz.'

'I don't mean this, I mean that.'

'The commercial?'

'Yes. What's it for?'

'Don't know, but whatever it is, I want some.'

'Mmmm. Nice.'

'What? That?'

'No, Jonny. Not that. This!'

On the telly, the bird has invited the fellow inside, with many a nudge, nudge, wink, wink, closing the door with the finest leer I have seen since I was last at Stratford.

Liz and I are getting well away, when this voice booms out of the set, which is now simply showing a bedroom door.

'Are you getting a job with the right sort of connections? Are you?'

I'm on the verge of getting the right sort of connection, but I'm not finding it hard work. Quite soft, in fact. But the voice makes an impression on me. So the ad is for some kind of work!

'If you want a job that'll give you some interesting openings, then make your connection with us. Have you got the nerve for it?'

I reckon they've been reading my books to steal for the script. All this about openings. They'll be on about unusual positions next. And do I have the nerve.

'If all this is for you, then apply tomorrow for a job as a gas fitter.'

'A gas fitter!'

Liz sits up and laughs. 'Sounds right for you, Jonny. Lots

of chances to meet ladies. And all those connections. But do you have the nerve?'

I show her in no uncertain terms. Tomorrow can wait until tomorrow.

Incidentally, before we slip easily into the next chapter and tomorrow, I suppose you know what the definition of nerve is?

It's crapping on someone's front step and then ringing the bell to ask if you can borrow some toilet paper!

See you tomorrow.

Chapter Five

Today is the tomorrow that you were so worried about yesterday.

Nothing like a bit of homespun rubbish to start a new chapter. I reckon if I work at it I could become the Pam Ayres of Great Barr.

> I wish I was a hedge-hopper,
> Life would be a farce.
> I'd climb up all the highest trees,
> And slide down on my hands and knees.

That wasn't the last line you expected, was it? You naughty people.

Still, you never get just what you expect. I have this mate who fancies himself as a pop guitarist, so he gets a job as a roadie, gigging round with some of the top groups. Helping set up the gear and break it down afterwards. That very hot summer it was.

That was the time there were millions of wasps and lady-birds and all that flying around the place. I remember he tells me about this one concert out in the country where he spends the whole afternoon pulling flies off Wings.

It will come as a great surprise to those of you who think they're reading *The Lion's Paw* by Claud Bottom to discover that the job that Jonny is about to try is that of gasman. I know there is a subtle clue to this on the front cover, but you'd be amazed the ideas people get about what they read. I get lots of great letters from readers, and you'd be surprised how many of them ask if there is any link between me and some other writer. Timothy somebody or other.

There isn't.

Anyway, the morning after seeing this commercial, I rise early. Don't we all?

(Publisher's Note: No.)

Well, I rise early. Makes the blankets look like a tent. Liz would do well in the building trade, as she has a great talent for demolishing erections.

After a brief pause for pawing briefs, I decide that today is the day for trying the Gas Board for a job as management trainee, which means that I first have to train as a gas fitter.

As I look after my body, I reckon that I am fitter than most. So it should be a breeze. If it is then I shall be gone with the wind.

'Jonny?'

'Oh, no. Here we go again. Liz has that look on her face that means 'I am about to give you some news that you are not going to like but I am wearing this expression in an attempt to soften the blow.'

I have been softened by blows before now, so I suppose that one more or less won't make an awful lot of difference. It can't be *that* bad.

'What is it, love?'

'I've got something to tell you.'

What did I tell you.

'What's that, love?'

Notice how calm I am remaining. But I have known Liz for quite a long time and she is always off on the move. I reckon she moves more than Pickfords.

'I'm very pleased that you're going to go out and get a job.'

'Yes.'

'I'm happy for you to stay here in this flat as long as I don't need it to myself or . . . anything.'

'Like shacking up with someone else?'

'Yes. Wouldn't have put it quite like that, but you were always short and to the point.'

'To the point, yes. Short, no.'

She laughs. 'At the moment the only person I'd like to shack up with is you, Jonny.'

'But?'

'But what?'

I am still in bed after the demolition bit, wondering if it's actually a good day for getting up and throwing on a few clothes. Liz has thrown on that t-shirt from San Francisco, and nearly missed.

I reach out and take her hand, rubbing a thoughtful first finger up and down the inside of her wrist. Never fails, does that.

'Jonny. Don't. You know I can't stand it when you do that. I go all weak and my legs forget that they're supposed to be my best friends.'

'You mean that even the best friends must part.'

'Yes. That's exactly it, love. I know we've only just got back together again, but I think we might soon be parted.'

My first thought is for poor Edgar. Having been out in the cold for longer than a Hull trawler, he has just enjoyed the first up and under for weeks.

Days actually, but it seems like weeks.

'Where are you going?'

I nearly add 'my pretty maiden,' but I resist the temptation.

'I've applied ages ago for a chance to do a three month course in creative writing up at Aberdeen.'

'Aberdeen!'

'Why not?'

'I thought the only writing up there was on the side of herring boxes.'

'Well you thought wrong, Jonathan May. And I've been accepted.'

'Creative writing! What do you want to learn to write?'

'I don't know.' There is a note of the old acid creeping in and I see this is not a good topic. A bounty, or even a mars, but not a topic.

'All right, Liz. I'm not my lover's keeper.'

She kisses me, and Edgar perks up. This is one of the perks of being Jonny May.

'I have to go in a couple of days. You'll stay on and keep an eye on the flat for me?'

'You think I want to be out on the streets?'

'No.'

'Then I'll keep an eye on the flat for you. Keep the bed warm.'

She wags a warning finger at me. A warning that is weakened by a giggle as I shove a toe which boldly goes where no toe has been before.

'Not *too* warm, my love.'

'Come on, Liz. I know very well that the moment you hit the streets of old Aberdeen you'll be ferreting around under the first kilt you see.'

She grins in that wicked manner she has. 'Maybe you're right at that. Can't wait to get my teeth into a braw bit o' sporran.'

'I hope it gives you indigestion,' I reply. 'I don't know what you want to go all the way up there for.'

'Why?'

'Well,' I say, putting her hand where it can do most good. 'You can toss my caber any day and I'll be coming through the rye.'

'You shouldn't eat so much porridge, Jonny.'

'You know what they do at a Quaker dance, don't you?' I

ask her, trying to hide my broken heart behind a laughing mask.

'No. Go on.'

'Twice round the floor and then outside . . .'

'For your oats.'

'Right.'

You're right.

I'm left.

She's gone.

She rings up this college place in Scotland, and they tell her she can start right away. So she leaves within about ten minutes, leaving me with a quick peck on the cheek and a strange case of the empty bed blues.

I must now try and pick up the pieces.

But first I shall have to have some food.

Those of you who are weak-stomached or of a nervous disposition are advised to leave the book at this point and rejoin it in a page or so.

The rest of you will enjoy another sample page from Jonny's Cook-Book.

(Publisher's Note: I'm afraid that I must leave you at this section as I have become quite ill in the past from simply reading Mister May's self-styled recipes. I hope you can manage without me for a while.)

If his wife can, then I reckon we can.

Fortunately, Liz keeps her kitchen well-stocked with all the essentials.

So does my old mum. But in her case the essentials include a fire-extinguisher, hammer and chisel and a copy of *Antidotes To Food-Poisoning For Home And Country.*

Take three slices of white bread. Three eggs. One tin of baked beans. From Heinz, and this is positively my last plug for them unless I get some freebies. That tin of beans should be a large tin, of course. For variation, you can always try the ones with little sausages in them.

Heat up some fat in a frying-pan until it is fairly hot. Start to boil the eggs. Put them in cold water and then bring to the boil slowly. The moment they start to boil properly time them for three minutes. That way you get nice firm whites and runny yolks. And I'm not yolking.

Put the beans into a saucepan, having first taken them out of the tin. Well, you never know. Heat slowly.

Now things are beginning to happen. Like the beans sticking and the eggs splitting. Drop the bread into the fat and squidge it around so that it soaks up plenty of hot fat. Not too hot or they'll go all crispy.

Turn them over in a few seconds so that both sides of the bread get soggy. Take out of frying-pan and place on plate. Pour over baked beans in liberal quantities. Liberal quantities means enough to satisfy Cyril Smith.

Take the eggs out after three minutes and shell in cold water. No!! Put the eggs in cold water, not yourself!

Place one soft-boiled egg on each mountain of beans and bread. So that they look like three great big steaming boils on your plate. Salt and pepper well.

Take up knife and fork. Be warned. You may need a spoon at the end.

Eat.

That'll put a golden lining on your stomach and let you face the world with a brave smile. Not to mention agonising gut-rot.

Seriously though, folks, I want you to know most sincerely what a truly wonderful meal that is, and the acid indigestion is just for fun.

Those of you who took the coward's way out and stopped reading may now come back and rejoin us. And that includes my cowardly Publisher. He's really a nice person, but he's just a bit immature. Young for his years. I'm younger than him, but I have this amazing maturity which so perfectly accompanics my natural charm and modesty. Compared to me he's an adolescent.

You know the definition of adolescence? It's what comes between puberty and adultery.

I go to the wardrobe and take out my cleanest dirty shirt. Put on my *New Riders Of The Purple Sage* t-shirt and a pair of trousers best suited to an interview for a job. One of Levi Strauss's best.

Don't think I only have one pair of jeans to my name. I have three. One on, one off and one in the wash.

Polish my boots to a dull gleam. Think about having a shave.

That's all I do. Just think about having a shave.

Well, I have one last night before we start watching the telly. Liz hates getting a nasty rash from my chin. Makes sitting down so uncomfortable. Whoooops! Let slip one of our favourite pleasures there. Still, it's always on the tip of my tongue.

And it's delicious!

The offices of the Gas Board nearest to me in Notting Hill are listed in the paper, as part of this massive advertising campaign. The picture in the paper is the same lady as on telly, dressed the same. For those of you who can't remember, and for Elias Banglestein, I shall mention it again.

In this picture she is posing provocatively on a big sofa, resting one hand on a gas oven. The housecoat is open further than it was on telly. Put it like this: If she was in danger of a cold on the chest on telly, then in the paper she's in greater danger of icicles from the roof of her passion palace.

There's the black bra which shows even more of the milk shakers. The stockings, knickers and the suspenders. Her legs are fairly well open, but the fellows who designed the ad are very subtle. I mean that her legs aren't open *quite* wide enough for a double-decker tram.

The words say: 'Everything gets done that much quicker with Gas. And I do mean *everything.*'

See what I mean about subtlety!

But it works with me. I can't wait to go and learn how to fit something like that. And I do mean the stove.

So here I am all dressed up and somewhere to go. If you can hold yourself in check – or in stripes for all I care, love – then I shall reveal more or less all in the next chapter.

Until then . . .

(Publisher's Note: Oh. Oh, oh, oh!! That fried bread and the eggs and . . . Excuse me, I think I'm going . . .)

If it was a gangster film he'd be retching for the sky.

Little one to tide you over the interminable delay between this page and the next one.

My success with ladies is partly due to my clothes. I dress very well.

And very quickly.

Chapter Six

I march into this great big office block with a brass plate outside telling me that I am in the right place to apply for a job with the Gas Board. It is the middle of the afternoon.

As I walk into the reception area I hear one of those loudspeaker things giving everyone in the works a time-check.

'For all workers, the time is three o'clock. For all of our brothers in the Common Market, the correct time is fifteen hundred hours.' A long pause. 'And for the directors and managers, the big hand is on the twelve and the little hand is on the three.'

There is a desk marked 'Enquiries' and I go to it, smiling in a friendly manner at the elderly lady behind it.

She recoils faster than a nine inch mortar.

And if you think that I'm going to make any reference to the way some ladies react when they see my own nine inch mortar, then you're quite right. Some of them recoil right back into the bed.

'Who are you?'

'I'm May,' I reply, feeling the sinking in the guts that means either I have eaten too much of the fried bread etc., or that the most repeated joke in history is about to get another airing.

'May what?' she asks.

I was right. It is the seventeenth time that this particular joke has appeared in the books of Jonathan May. But I can't help it. This really is what people say to me.

I suppose it could be worse.

'What's your name?'

'I'm Mumble.'

'Well, you ought to speak up then.'

Or: 'What's your name?'

'I'm Asturbate.'

'Well, you ought to stop it or you'll go blind and deaf.'

Back to the Gas offices and the old lady with the enquiring sign on her desk.

'No. Not May what. My name is Jonathan May and I've come in response to the advert.'

'I'm sorry.'

'What for?'

'I don't know what floor.'

'Floor?'

'More what?'

I'm not sure if it's me going loony or her.

She is looking at me very suspiciously. Like I've marched into a meeting of the National Front singing the 'Red Flag'.

So I'll try again. If at first you don't succeed, then get some other sucker to have a go. But there's nobody else there.

'I want a job.'

Suddenly I spot that she has a chunk of pink plastic shoved in her ear-hole and a microphone pinned to the front of her dress. For a moment I wonder if this can be the dreaded Jonathan Routh with his 'Candid Camera'. Surely no organisation is going to be so ridiculous as to put a poor deaf lady on their Enquiries Desk.

Well done the Gas Board! Sarcastic rounds of applause and false congratulations.

'Could you speak up, young man. I'm afraid that I'm a little hard of hearing.'

That's like saying that in their day the Beatles weren't a bad pop music group.

'I want to do a job!'

She looks concerned. 'Dear, dear. Big job or little job?'

'Eh?'

'Do you want number ones or number twos? There's a toilet over there, but it gets very busy if you want to do big jobs, you see.'

She is rather like what you get to see when you fly over Egypt in an aeroplane.

See Nile.

'Work. Me wantum work. Plenty job with heap big pile of wampum endum weekum.'

'Miss Gabbitas-Thring is in charge of management training in the Personnel Offices on the ninth floor.'

The voice comes from behind me. The old lady at the desk has resumed her somnolent posture. I saw that in a book once. It means that she's falling asleep again.

I'm glad to be able to stop talking in that mock Sitting Bull voice. I've always had reservations about Indians!

The owner of the voice is a glad sight on the eye, and I give her the benefit of the full-power, halogen-quartz, Jonny May smile, Grade A.

To her great credit, she hardly flinches, though her own smile wavers at the edges.

Even a wavering smile from such a pretty thing is better than no smile at all. She is tiny, standing not more than five feet tall in a pair of stiletto-heeled shoes with ankle straps, the like of which I have not seen since I was a tiny toddler and the Teds ruled West Bromwich with their velvet collars and winkle-pickers.

Aside from the shoes she is dressed quite demurely. Mid-thigh blue skirt and a white blouse unbuttoned to show a touch of cleavage. About the same amount that Angela Rippon shows when she's feeling specially daring. The lady – in the Gas offices, not the exquisite Angie – has blonde hair cropped short. Her eyes are as blue as the mould on a ripe cheese. I know that's not flattering but that's the shade I mean. You might get a load of rubbish from Jonny May, but you can be guaranteed that it's honest rubbish. I could have said that her eyes were the shade of blue of the sea boiling around the jagged rocks of Ibiza. Which they may be, but I've never been there.

'Are you going to train as a fitter?'

I nod. 'Yes. And thanks for telling me where to go. Do you work here?'

'Not at the moment. But I've just been up in Personnel and I start as a trainee fitter on Monday next.'

'To see Mrs . . . what did you say her name was?'

'Gabbitas-Thring.'

'You saw her?'

'Yes. You're going up for the same job, are you, Mister . . . I don't know your name.'

I avoid *the* joke.

'I'm called Jonathan May. I hope we both get started together.'

'Cheeky fellow.'

'I know. I am awful, but I like me.'

She laughs. Get them laughing and you're at least halfway there.

Behind the desk the old lady has fallen asleep, snoring away fit to wake Concorde. That's fair enough. Concorde wakes lots of people anyway.

'What's your name?' I ask the vision of beauty, both Edgar and I finding our hopes rising at the thought that sexual equality has reached gas fitters. Maybe she and I will end up making our connections together.

'I'm called Mandy Ranndee.'

There's no answer to that, is there? Why can't I meet a

nice girl with a nice ordinary name? Like Mary Brown or Ann Smith. Funnily enough, I did once go out for a time with a smashing bird called Ann Smith. Flew off to America and became an air-hostess.

Must be careful with a name like Mandy Ranndee. Mustn't let my tongue slip or you never know where it might end up.

'Maybe I'll see you next week, Mandy?'

'Yes, Jonny. That'd be nice. Hope the interview goes well for you. From what I saw of Mrs Gabbitas-Thring, I think you shouldn't find it too hard to get on with her.'

'What do you mean by "too hard", Mandy?'

She laughs. 'Wait till you see her. And then see how hard it is.'

She gives me a wave and walks off out of the main door into the sunshine, her high heels clicking and clacking like a fiesta of flamenco dancers. Very pretty little lady, Miss Ranndee. Wonder if she is.

I watch her going, and find the prospect attractive. If she looks like that when she's going, I wonder what she'll be like coming?

On I go to Personnel. The last time I went to a Personnel Department it was the infamous Stoppers of Knightsbridge, with the even more infamous Harknett sisters. Wonder what happened to them. Haven't seen any remakes of *Cinderella* lately.

(Publisher's Note: Psssst!)

Take no note of him. He's probably been out for one of his lunches and got psssst again.

Talking about *Cinderella* I will give you a genuine and useless piece of information. In the original German version of the story the Ugly Sisters try so hard to get their feet into the glass slipper that they go to the lengths of cutting off their own toes.

Unfunny but true.

The way the Harknett sisters walked around Stoppers store

I reckon there was something not quite right with their plates of meat.

(Publisher's Note: Pssssstt! Mister May. Will you take this opportunity for a plug?)

Right. I'll have a square-pin thirteen amp if it's all the same to you.

(Publisher's Note: No. A plug for the book about Stoppers of Knightsbridge. We've overprinted and got thousands left in the warehouse and . . . Oooh. What a giveaway. I mean there are just one or two copies left so encourage folks to hurry up and get them.)

All right. The Harknetts appear in *Confessions Of A Shop Assistant*, the first of my hilarious adventures, about my very first job when I come down to London from Birmingham. You know about Birmingham? It's the city where they pull down lovely old buildings to make roads to encourage cars. Then they make all the roads one-way to discourage all the cars.

The smiling lift-attendant takes me to the right floor for the Personnel Department, and I walk along the corridor, looking for the room.

Here it is.

'Knock and Enter.'

I knock.

And enter.

I admit that my knees are trembling a bit. Nothing like a bit of knee-trembler, is there, Missus?

Last time I got involved with such a lady was not happy. You can read all about this in *Confessions Of A Shop* . . . Oh, sorry. Just done that bit. But Miss Harknett was a sight to terrify even a Pontypool prop forward.

She had thighs like oak trees, and a waist as big as all outdoors. She had so much five o'clock shadow that it used to appear at four o'clock. Nobody could be quite like that.

Well . . . .

Mrs Gabbitas-Thring is not *quite* like that. Her thighs are smaller than oak trees. More like very large willows. The sight of them makes me weep anyway. And she doesn't need to shave today. By the stubble I would guess she shaved yesterday.

'Who are you?' she booms with a noise like the *QE2* sailing into New York Harbour.

Not to be caught out for a second time in the same day, I reply carefully.

'I'm Mister Jonathan May and I have come in response to your advertisements in the newspapers and on the television.'

'So you're another of the dirty-minded little oiks conned by that slut in the black knickers! !'

By Tone E. Hatch! But I am not having that sort of insult. Who does she think she is?

'Who do you think you are?'

'I've told you. I've come about the job of trainee manager with the . . .'

'Fitter?'

'Than I have been in years. But why . . .'

'Damn fool. The job says management trainee, but it's really for gas fitters. There's a shortage at the moment as the conversions increase.'

'Yes. My Aunt Rose nearly became a Catholic. It was at this meeting in Cannon Hill Park and . . .'

'Were you born an idiot? Or have you worked hard all your life at it?'

'Why?'

'Gas conversions, laddy. I'm talking about gas conversions. Still, despite your obvious stupidity, you seem to be fairly healthy. Fill that form in on the desk.'

I start away, writing down the usual old rubbish. I reckon that they must have a special department in some Ministry or other where very old men in a fusty room make them up, taking care that no new questions shall ever appear on application forms. Except maybe once every fifty years.

'Albert?'

'Yes, Cyril.'

'Fifty years. I suggest we remove the question about numbers of servants in parents' house.'

'But what shall we put in its place?'

'All officers and positions held at all schools, including Junior and Infants.'

We fade away from the room leaving these two old nits clapping their wrinkled hands.

These forms really are a bleeding waste of time. Why do they want to know nationality of grandparents?

The only question I'm never sure about is the one that simply says 'Sex?'

I always write down: 'Yes.'

Despite the rude way she comes on when I walk in her office, Mrs Gabbitas-Thring seems to be really quite friendly when you get to know her.

In fact, she is becoming *very* friendly.

If she wasn't built like the Incredible Hulk with B.O. to match, I wouldn't mind. The fact that she is old enough to be my mum is neither here nor there. But it *is* 'there'.

She is standing behind me, running her hand gently across the top of my locks. Reading the answers on my application form.

'So young. Such a good place, Birmingham, I always think.'

Her fingers have reached the inside of my collar and she seems to be intending to go further. I shuffle in my seat. I know that I want this job quite badly, but I'm beginning to wonder about the price that I'm going to be expected to pay for the privilege.

'Jonathan. That's a nice name. I knew a little Jonny once.'

'I knew a very chubby Fanny once, but I'm not boasting about it.'

She slaps me in a saucy manner on the back, nearly knocking me clean into the middle of the next chapter. When Mrs

Gabbitas-Thring laughs, it sounds like sulphur dioxide bubbling through warm tar.

'Cheeky young blade, aren't you?'

'If I'm a blade, you can keep off my grass,' I reply wittily, worried at the way she is starting to let her ten pink soldiers go a'wondering among my pastures.

'There's not a lot of difference in our ages, really, you know.'

No more than between any average healthy young lad and his grandmother.

'Many men have told me that I have both the face and body of a girl of seventeen,' says Mrs Gabbitas-Thring, simpering like a drunk debutante.

Not a pretty sight.

'Well you better give them back. They're getting awfully wrinkled,' I say.

Very quietly.

Like I tell you, I want this job.

'It rests with me whether or not you get this job, you know?'

Do I believe her, or do I call her bluff?

'If you play ball with me, Jonny, then I'm sure I'll enjoy playing with your . . .'

'No!'

'What do you mean by that?' she thunders, looming over me like the Rock of Gibraltar. I haven't seen a frontage like that since Sabrina first appeared on telly. Every time she moved on the goggle-box even the plaster ducks on our wall ducked.

Maybe ducks don't duck. Maybe they people. 'Hey, Donald Duck. People! Whoops. Too late.'

'Nothing. Just that . . .'

'Mister May, I suggest that if I am prepared to scratch yours, then you should be prepared to scratch mine.'

'But mine doesn't itch,' I say plaintively, looking longingly at the door out of the office and wondering if it's all worth it. There must be a way out. And I'm *not* talking about the office! I'm talking about getting away from Bride of Godzilla and still getting the job.

It's a problem that demands a man with the highest qualities of cunning and intelligence. Who else but . . . ?

'Mister May?'

She is leaning across the desk, eyes blazing like a Welsh preacher fighting against Sunday opening. To my horror, her fingers are beginning to unbutton the top of her blouse. Already I am beginning to feel like I do at school when they show us a film of the Grand Canyon with its heaving boulders and deep cracks.

From what I can see of Mrs Gabbitas-Thring, it is not only her boulders that will heave, and her cracks are likely to be exceedingly deep. Short of tying my ankles to the legs of the desk, I am not sure what I can do.

'Will you play ball with me?'

'Will you give me the job?'

She smiles. A vast vision which is like a murky sun rising over the Corporation rubbish dump. She clearly thinks she has me by the short and curlies.

Incidentally. Have any of you ever been picked up by the fuzz?

Hurts, doesn't it?

After I have promised to do what she wants, Mrs Gabbitas-Thring signs my application form and gives it back to me, making sure that she is well between the door and me. As the lady is built like a brick privy, there is not much chance of running past her. About as much chance as Chelsea winning anything other than a spoon made out of wood. Or as much chance as me ever liking the Bay City Rollers.

'Now,' she says, beginning the unbuttoning for the second time.

Is this the end?

(Publisher's Note: I'm afraid not, and it's rather naughty

of Mister May to raise your hopes like that.)

His hopes are about all he's raised in the last ten years!

From the fact we aren't even halfway through the book, I suppose I can't hope to create panic and consternation among you readers. Obviously your hero would never sell out to such a dreadful extent. Never use his marvellous body and skill at thingie just to help get a job.

Well, he would if it wasn't anyone looking quite as horrible as Mrs Gabbitas-Thring. I'm not saying she's got bad body odour. To say that would mean opening my mouth and I might inhale it and pass out.

So, how am I going to avoid this fate worse than death? Well may you ask.

'I'm ready,' I say, feeling the application form safely in the right pocket of my denim jeans.

She licks her lips. I have not seen such eager anticipation since the West Indies' fast bowlers were getting stuck into England batsmen.

The blouse is open nearly to the waist, and I can see a vast expanse of liberty-bodice and a bra that looks more of a miracle of engineering than the Forth Bridge. The colour of her once-white underwear reminds me of a famous novelist. Grey and green.

And if you don't get it, then I'm sorry, but I'm not going to explain it. Don't worry, anyway, I am about to reveal all about Mrs Gabbitas-Thring.

I get my words in just before she reveals all, stopping her in her tracks like a rabbit picked off by a twelve-bore. If you've never heard of a twelve-bore, then you've never talked with a dozen Brummies.

'Mrs Gabbitas-Thring?'

'What is it, you tantalising young man?'

'They'll want your address.'

'Yes. Of course, you ravishing . . . Who will want my address?'

'The clinic.'

'The clinic??'

This is delivered in a voice like the late great Edith Evans saying 'A handbag!!' in that Oscar Wilde film.

'*The* clinic.' I rub the side of my nose with a cautionary finger, feeling like an Arab pimp selling dirty postcards in an old bazaar in Cairo.

'I don't understand.' But she has stopped her advance and is nervously fumbling at the busty covering as though she might be having second thoughts. Or even third ones.

'The special clinic. The Martha and Luke Clinic. The Private Clinic. The Adam and Eve Clinic. The Nudge Nudge Clinic. The . . . '

'You don't mean . . . !!!!!!'

Mrs Gabbitas-Thring could not look more shocked if I'd suggested that Sacha Distel wears a wig. Not that I am suggesting that, of course.

'Yes. That's what I mean.'

She gets the message. The good lady knows the kind of clinic I mean, and I reckon you do too. Not that any of you upright people will have ever been there. And if you stay upright then the chances are a bit less that you've been there.

And to stop you writing in, I haven't either. I was just there to wait for a friend.

Honest.

'Get out!'

'I thought you wanted a bit of the other.'

'Oooooh. I think I'm going to faint.'

She feints to the left and then the right, but finally subsides into a big chair like an oil tanker being launched sideways down the Clyde.

I give her a smile and bow, making sure the signed application form is still safely in my pocket.

'I shall have to have everything disinfected as soon as you have gone,' she moans.

'Everything?' I ask, with a meaningful wink. Like someone who got a bit tiddly at a party and is chatting up the wife of the host. Sort of a tiddly-wink.

She groans again, and flaps her hands at the air like she just dropped a cheesy thumper and is trying to waft it away before anyone notices.

I am away, closing the door gently behind me, ready to begin work at the training centre on Monday, where I hope to also start work on the delicious Mandy Ranndee.

The week-end is a boring and lonely time, so to keep us both going, here's a little memory of times past. What some poet I read at school called a memory of times past, not worth forgetting. It's a bit embarrassing, but I always give you the hole truth, even if it makes me look a bit of a berke.

Here it is. After it's over, we shall be magically transported to Monday and the training place. See you there.

It's thinking about Mrs Gabbitas-Thring waving her hand like that reminds me of it. If I've ever told you about this, I'm sorry. But it proves I'm consistent.

It's a couple of years back while I'm still in the land of busy roads and empty larders. Of course. Birmingham.

I'm going out with a bird called Loony June, on account of she doesn't have quite all her marbles. But what she does have makes up for that. Who listens to the mantelpiece when they're poking the fire, I always say?

And June has taken me home to meet her family, who live in a classy part of Birmingham called Edgbaston. You pronounce the 'ba' part of the word like you're doing a great sheep impression, and not like you're impersonating Eddie Waring. Who some find wearing, but not me.

Anyway, there we all are with cups balanced on our knees, enjoying cucumber sandwiches. As if anyone could actually enjoy such things. Her old man is some kind of accountant, and her mum is a leading Tory. All gin, tonics and big hats. Who talks about nothing but hanging, trade unions and repatriation for the blacks. Her favourite nightmare is about being murdered by a West Indian shop steward.

I'm having a bit of trouble having had my usual baked beans lunch, and to try to keep people's minds off the odd odour, I start a conversation about morality.

I like that bloke Cyril Fletcher and his 'Odd Odours', don't you.

'I tell the tale of Edward Plumb, who stuck a doughnut up his bum. To ease himself he tried to ram, a finger up, got in a jam.' You know the sort of thing.

This chat about morality goes well, helped by her old man bringing out a couple of magnums of his peas' pod and kipper bone wine. Which is also used as paint stripper. I knocked back a glass or two before I find that I am well newted, and find it difficult to behave properly.

At some point in the conversation, her old man gets very serious, making it clear that he is regarding me as a prospective son-in-law. Though his wife doesn't seem to agree.

I hear her whisper to him over the chinking of stale Eccles cakes: 'If he marries our June, you won't be losing a daughter. You'll be gaining an idiot.'

But still the talk flows on, and I find it harder and harder to keep my self-control.

'Jonny.'

'Yes, sir.' The 'sir' always goes down well with birds' parents.

'You know that I place great importance on sexual morals? You know that?'

'I didn't, but I do now, sir.'

'I can sit here and say that I never slept with another woman until I married June's mother. When the day comes, will you be able to say that to your own children?'

'Yes,' I reply. 'But not with such a straight face.'

Chapter Seven

I get to the wrong room, at the wrong time. But fortunately I am early rather than late so I manage to get to the right room for the first lecture of the day. My new job has begun.

Before I tell you a bit about that first day, I should tell you that the entire May family has trouble with getting things right. I remember the time that my dear sister Melanie, who makes Lucrezia Borgia seem like Florence Nightingale, goes to the doctor because she wants a little check-up. She has this thing about East European midgets.

Actually, she goes in the surgery, and the doctor tells her to take all her clothes off. If you met my sister Melanie, and you were a fellow between eleven and the cemetery, you'd probably want her to take all her clothes off as well.

She does it and he asks her to bend over the end of the couch while he takes her temperature.

'Right over, please.'

'Is that far enough?'

'No. More please.'

'Is that far enough?'

'Yes.'

'Oooooooooooh !!!!'

'What is wrong, Miss May?'

'You've got that bleedin' thermometer in the wrong place, doctor.'

He laughs. 'That is where you are wrong, Miss May. Doubly wrong.'

'What?'

'Firstly it is not a thermometer, and secondly I assure you that it *is* in the right place.'

In point of fact, we are now just about up to where I was at the beginning of the book. But I always like to give you plenty of background. So here I am, ready to learn all about being a gasman.

As I think I might have mentioned, the person who is to show me all about connections and joints and how to fill a soggy socket, is a lovely lady.

More of her later.

But not much later so don't go too far away.

You might also be interested in the rest of the class, including Miss Ranndee.

Even if you're not, I'm going to tell you about them.

If you can remember that far back, you will recall that the lady instructor rejoices in the name of Tracey Tyttefiedler. And I'm still not going to tell you how she pronounces her name.

There are eight of us in the class. Starting at the top, with me. Five other blokes, most of them round about twenty. And a couple of birds. To put you out of your misery, one of them is the tiny Miss Ranndee. The other is a girl called Polly Inger.

She is not a pretty Polly.

I've had several blind dates in my time, where a mate says his bird's got this friend who'd like to meet you. You know what I mean? Your mate's girl looks like something out of the pages of *Men Only* while you end up with something out of *Pig-breeders' Monthly*.

This is Polly. She seems a nice friendly girl, but she is what mothers would call 'homely'. While Mandy is the sort of girl that mothers would hate and dads would go bananas over.

I'm not sure about Tracey Tyttefiedler. She's quite tall, and has a body like a well-built amusement park. Lots of attractions to keep you going all day. Her hair's what might best be termed an unnatural blonde. You can see that when you get to the roots of the problem. She wears some sort of uniform, which consists of a dark blue sweater and a dark blue skirt. It is obvious that the Gas people were badly stocked on uniforms when Tracey came along.

The jumper would be a tight fit on Jane Birkin and the skirt would be short on Barbara Windsor. On Tracey the effect is amazing and the collective blood-pressure of every man in the room rises as she walks in. It's not just the blood-pressure that rises, either. I've not seen such a shuffling on seats and adjusting of trousers since Keith Williams got busy with the itching powder during French one hot June afternoon.

My Publisher asks me to tell you as much as possible about the way they train gas fitters and conversion engineers, as he reckons that all readers would find it interesting. Having done the job I can tell you that it is about as interesting as doing paper folding with wet cardboard.

There's only a limited number of types of appliance with which we have to deal, and there's a booklet on each of them. Telling you what part you need and what you have to do with it. Since I have never had any trouble about knowing what to do with all of my parts it is a doddle.

So, I shall not try to bore you with loads of technical guff. All you need to know is that most of the lectures are about how to convert ovens and fires and fridges and old boilers to natural gas. The mention of old boilers makes me wonder if Mrs Gabbitas-Thring had yet been converted.

We are also taught how to detect leaks, which is very useful if you happen to be living in Wales. And how to cure these leaks. There is also one talk on: 'What to do to try and stop the customers from complaining so often.'

The lovely Miss Tyttefiedler has us in her hot little hands for four lectures a day. This lasts two weeks at the end of which we are tested to see if we are ready to don the uniform and go out on the road with an experienced fitter as a sort of apprenticeship.

I spend much of this fortnight trying to strike up a closer aquaintanceship with Mandy. I do not get very far. Not even above knee-level, though she is not unfriendly. By that I mean that she keeps on smiling, even while she's crossing her legs on your fingers.

Polly is a different problem. I have to work hard at keeping Edgar out of her clutches. She has more clutches than a barnful of battery hens. Funnily enough, when it comes to being tested on our work and on what we've learned, Polly comes second in the group.

I know it's not very gentlemanly, but Jonny May comes first. I believe in always trying my best to come first in everything I do.

Nearly everything.

After me and Polly come four other blokes and then Mandy propping up the list. She only just scrapes through at the end.

Ah, you say. Not to mention, ha. Jonny has slipped up. Made a bloomer. Dropped a bit of a whoopsie. Can't count.

The very idea. I am known as the Count of Monty Modlyn.

When I tell you how many there are in our little group, I should have told you that I am not the only one there from Birmingham. The eighth person is another Brummie. While Jonny May is not the typical Brummie, in that he can walk and chew gum at the same time, Ebenezer Mole-Strangler is a fine representative of the second city in the land.

His old man, Jeroboam Mole-Strangler, was Birmingham's one and only kamikaze pilot during the war. He flew one hundred and fourteen unsuccessful missions.

We're having a bit of a chat one afternoon waiting for Miss Tyttefiedler to arrive – notice that I didn't say 'come' – and the subject of religion is being discussed. Ebenezer is sitting there listening and suddenly he interrupts us.

'Here,' he says. 'I always thought that a religious movement was what you got when you crossed holy water and prune juice.'

You will not be that surprised to learn that Ebenezer does not manage to pass the final exam, and it is not that hard. Though I admit that it might task the brain-power of a mentally-deficient orang-outang.

It starts off by saying 'Do not write on both sides of the paper at once.'

And you have to select the right answer to some questions from a lot of possibilities. Not that challenging.

For instance.

'You are making a call on a customer who has made nineteen previous requests for service. You yourself have promised on no less than eleven occasions to arrive promptly and you have never yet turned up. A week earlier you promised a service call for the afternoon of Monday. On the Wednesday morning after, knowing that the lady will have taken the whole of Monday off work with consequent loss of earnings, you drive past her house, stopping only to push a card through her door saying that you called as requested but obtained no reply. On finally being confronted by the angry customer, which of the following excuses would you use to try and pacify her?'

And there is this list of possible excuses below. You have to tick the one you think is best; Ebenezer ticks them all, including his own name and the date.

1. The van broke down.
2. Didn't you get the call saying we wouldn't come on Monday?

3. It's holidays.
4. We couldn't get the parts.
5. We couldn't get the parts.
6. We couldn't get the parts.
7. I had a headache.
8. We couldn't get the parts.
9. Strike at the works.
10. Oh, that bloody silly girl in the office! She's always getting messages wrong.
11. Yeah. It's a sod, innit?
12. It's the wrong time of month for me.
13. We still couldn't get the parts.
14. I've just had my hair done.
15. The relief van broke down.
16. I called and got no answer.
17. You'll wake the children.
18. We're still trying to get the parts.
19. Sorry.
20. Not me, lady. Must have been one of our other fitters you spoke to.

I'm not going to tell you what the right answer is. You have to guess. Anyway, like I say, I manage to get top marks, which isn't that great when you consider the quality of the opposition. It's like Magnusson Magnussonsonson, or whatever his name is, versus Eccles.

But I do have a few problems with some of the practical tests. If you glance back to the first five pages of this most wonderful book, you'll see the kind of thing I mean.

On the last afternoon, Tracey Tyttefiedler sends all the rest of the group over to the canteen for a break. And a Kit-Kat for all I know.

'Jonny?'

'Yes, Tracey.' We're very informal here, you notice. None of that 'Mister' and 'Mrs' rubbish. Though some people like the programme, I'm told.

'I'd like you to stay behind for an hour while we try and get your connections tightened up a bit. The last one was very loose and sloppy.'

'Right,' I say, cursing as this will mean a lost opportunity to chat up Mandy Ranndee before we hit the road, Jack.

Still, an hour alone with Tracey is better than a slap in the face with a wet haddock.

The door of the room shuts behind Polly, who gives me a last lingering look before leaving. You linger longer with a longer linger. Then the room is quiet.

'Come on, Jonny. Let's see if we can't get things in hand and make a start. You'll need this sort of skill when you're out on your own. I won't be at your elbow like I am here to tell you when to make it hard and when to put it in.'

She is now sitting on the seat, right by me, so that I can feel her arm against mine, and her leg brushing my thigh. If Edgar has anything to do with it, I am not going to need her to tell me when to make it hard and all that.

'Tracey. Can I tell you something?'

'Of course. I'll just get this warmed up. Roll it around in my fingers. What is it?'

'I think you're very attractive.'

'Oh.'

I follow up with the fingers along the inside of the wrist bit, and before you can say 'High Speed Gas', we are rolling around on the carpet.

'The door. Lock it.'

I am already about to shoot my bolt so I use the opportunity to walk stiff-legged across and slip the catch. As I turn round I see that Tracey is getting ready for action. The dark blue sweater has gone, and so has the skirt. My instructor is left wearing a white bra. Lacy Tracey. And a half-slip. Having slipped the catch I now catch the slip. Under it I can see that she wears the abominable tights. With a pair of white pants on top of them.

Interesting research to be done some time about why women choose to wear their knickers either over or under tights. I'm sure there's some deep psychological reason for it. Think about the girls you've known, fellows.

There are of course those rare birds that don't wear any at all. But some of them are just plain absent-minded. I remember Liz James telling me that she is once off to work and doesn't realise she's forgotten until she sits on the freezing cold concrete seat at the bus stop. A chilling prospect!

'Get them off, Jonny. Show me the equipment and I'll see if it's up to scratch.'

'It's up all right, but I don't want it scratched. Just a gentle rolling motion between fingers and thumb will do me just fine.'

'Ooooh. That'll do me fine, as well. Come on.'

Off fly my denims and jeans, followed very closely by the purple pants. Tracey has wriggled out of the bra, spilling her Colt forty-fives all over the place. Not really all over the place. But here and there. One here and the other there.

I find that I have two tongues in my mouth and only one of them is mine. And there is a hand caressing Edgar. And that hand isn't mine either. What is rubbing up against my lips isn't mine either. Unless I have been the victim of a strange operation.

'How's it coming, Jonny?'

I smile modestly.

'I'd still like to get my fingers round it and give it a feel to make sure it's hard enough.'

She gets her fingers round it and gives it a firm squeeze, like seeing if bananas are ripe enough. She seems pleased with the ripeness of my banana.

'Very good, Jonny. That's lovely and firm. Do be careful and don't let it get too hard. There's a real problem of getting it in if it's too hard.'

She's telling me.

(Publisher's Note: I have the oddest feeling that I've read all this before somewhere. Perhaps I'd better go and lie down until the feeling passes off.)

Now he's gone I can tell you that he's right. Tracey is using exactly the same chat for thingie as she does for instructions about mending leaky joints. Read the first few pages of this book if you don't believe me.

If you're in your garden and you get a leaky joint, it shows you ought to keep off the grass. Be a dope if you don't.

Back to Miss Tyttefiedler.

By now we are so close together that you couldn't get a copy of the Wit and Wisdom of Derek Hobson between us. I know I said Nicholas Parsons last time, but it's time we had a go at someone else.

We have come together a bit fast, and there is an entry problem.

'I think I'd rather you used some kind of grease. Makes the connection so much easier.'

'I'm all in favour of that, Tracey.'

Rather than use nasty sticky grease I apply a bit of spit and polish. Actually, I don't bother with the polish bit. Never liked Warsaw anyway.

The distraction distracts me, and Tracey notices a slight change.

'Leave it for too long and it goes soft and we know how much use that is. Don't we, Jonny?'

Feeling like a bailiff trying to evict a load of squatters, I carry on trying to force an entry.

'Right, Jonny. I think the time has come when you're going to have to really push it in. Don't be shy. Ram it in. Harder the better.'

When your lady instructor talks to you like that, then who am I to try and withdraw?

'Shouldn't you take your hands off it first?'

Tracey gives another of her special laughs. The sort that would make any vicar turn in his cassock.

'Yes. I suppose it might be easier. Now, off you go. Lovely. Great. Oh, Jonny. You're really very good at this, aren't you?'

I try and nod but find that my teeth are tangled up with her double barrels. And Miss Tyttefiedler has better double barrels than Worthingtons.

At this point, and it's rude to point, Edgar is going well and any similarity to any previous conversation comes to a sticky end.

Nothing like a sticky end, is there, Missus?

I wish that Miss Tyttefiedler would cut her nails, as she seems to be trying to turn my back into an aerial map of Spaghetti Junction. Some birds when you get near to the point of no-return start to make a lot of noise. I'm never sure if this is because they've read about other birds in books and magazines doing that, or whether it's all part of the big turn-on. I don't mind a few gasps and moans. Even a pant or two. But I can't stand the sort of lady who gives you a running commentary like she's talking about the end of an exciting horse-race.

'Yes. Up a . . . in with . . . harder on . . . ram the . . . give the . . . lick . . . both of . . . I want the . . .'

That sort of chat. Fortunately, Tracey is not that sort of talker at all and we end in an assortment of low groans and a lot of clutching and kissing. She gets more suction going than a factory full of vacuum cleaners and Edgar feels the great satisfaction of a job well done.

Trouble is after that you always feel like lying back and having a rest, but Miss Tyttefiedler has to go and get the loose ends tied up. I tuck away my loose end and start to get dressed.

'You'll be all right now when you come to getting it hard

and filling in the holes, won't you, Jonny?' says the instructor with a wicked grin.

Even an ordinary grin from a fanciable girl gets me started. When the grin turns out to be wicked, then I'm finished. Even if I have just finished I'm started again.

So we do.

'There. Thanks, Jonny. I don't think there's anything else I can teach you.'

If she's anything to go by, then I can only repeat what I said at the end of the first chapter about my new job. Like that leaping Mister Flash says: It's going to be a gas, gas, gas!

I have high hopes of the new job. You do know the definition of hope, of course?

No?

Well, hope is a man of ninety who gets married and starts looking for a house near a school.

Chapter Eight

I am on the job.

(Publisher's Note: Not for the first time. I didn't think he was ever going to get started!)

Isn't it funny how the things he moans to me about are just the same as his wife moans to me about. She also says he can't even finish when he does get started, but that's a different story.

I am on the early shift on Monday. I catch a glimpse of Mandy Ranndee, being whisked off by one of the older fitters who looks as if he can't believe his luck. Like a bloke who's stepped in a pile of cow's left-behinds and found a bunch of fivers hidden in it.

Polly stumps up in a pair of Wellingtons that looks as if they belonged to the grand old Duke himself. I don't envy the fitter who takes her out on the job. The others in my group all vanish and I am left waiting for my own man, feeling like a spare kick at a kung fu wedding.

Speaking of which, I wonder if I ever told you about the time that my Uncle Nick takes up Kunging and Fuing?

He's fed up of having the whatsits knocked out of him in the local boozer in West Bromwich. I'm not saying that Uncle

Nick isn't very tall, but even when he has a pee someone has to put him up to it.

You've got to realise that pubs in the Midlands aren't all soft like down south. I remember going in this bar in the quiet side of West Bromwich, which is the side where the police only have to go in fours. It's just on opening time and the landlord is standing behind the bar washing a glass. It seems quite pleasant, with fresh sawdust on the floor. I comment on this to the jovial mine host. Actually, he might be yours, but he certainly isn't mine.

'That's not blurry sawdust, you stupid bleeder,' he replies. 'That's blurry last night's blurry furniture!'

Anyway, back to Uncle Nick and his regular clobberings.

He goes to this Hong Kong fooey stuff for about six months, doing all the bowing and screaming. Punching and kicking and all that. Practises until he can break a pile of slates with his head and kick through a bundle of wood with his bare feet. This last is his favourite trick, and he can't wait until he goes back to his usual boozer and show them all his new skills. But specially where he splinters the wood with his bare feet.

First night there and the aggro starts, with a bunch of big navvies picking on him. Doesn't worry him at all. Reckons he can do the lot of them.

Only one thing wrong.

By the time he's got his shoes and socks off ready to clobber them, they've kicked the whatsits out of him.

'Hello sonny. Am I hurting you? I should be, I'm standing on your hair!!'

It can't be! This isn't the experienced fitter who will take me about with him for a few days showing me the ropes!

'Where's your handbag, sonny? Left it at home with your high-heels! Haw, haw, haw, haw, haw.'

If he shows me the ropes I reckon that I'll strangle him with them.

He's about five feet one tall, with shoulders like Mister Universe and a gut like my Uncle Angus. Face as red as a ruptured turkey. Nasty little moustache hanging under his nose as if he can't get rid of it. Like the one that actor who played the Inspector in 'On The Buses' had. Like an over-worked toothbrush.

I wonder why he bothers to cultivate it there when it grows wild round his . . .

(Publisher's Note: Sorry. Can't let you say that.)

What?

(Publisher's Note: That. The word you put there. That begins with 'a' and ends with 'e'.)

The only thing thicker than my Publisher is a Brummie. And the only thing thicker than a Brummie is two Brummies.

But back to my fitter, who is clearly going to be a right bundle of fun. Sort of like the Chancellor of the Exchequer but without his marvellous gift for knockabout comedy.

'Your name May?'

'Yes.'

'Bloody silly name. May what? Darling bloody buds of May? Haw, haw, haw!'

I'm the only one who makes jokes about my name. And if he carries on laughing like that I shall be quitting the Gas Board forthwith. Or even thirdwith. His laugh makes Margaret Powell sound like Caruso. It's the sort of high-pitched whine that breaks glass at fifty paces and makes your ears feel like they've been sand-blasted from the inside.

'I'm Mister Erry.'

'You're what?'

He looks like a disgruntled walrus. 'I said I'm Erry.'

'You don't look very merry to me.'

'Cheeky young bleeder. I'll . . .'

There comes a point, and I'm not talking about *that*, Missus. A point beyond which I don't let anyone push me around. And Mister Erry has long passed it.

'You'll do what, Smiley?' I ask him, flexing the muscles around and punching the right fist into the left palm as hard as I can. Makes a great noise.

Also hurts like Hell, but it's worth it for the effect you get.

'Listen, sonny. I've been doing this job for the last twenty years so don't try anything on with me.'

'All I'm saying is that I'm not going to put with any crap from you. And just because you've been doing the same job for that long don't think you've got the right to try and swing it over me. Right?'

He nods grudgingly. I know, and he knows that I know that all fitters are told they have to make every effort to get on well with the apprentice fitters and that there's a bonus scheme for those who do. And a black mark against those who don't.

'Tell you what. I'm Jonny.'

Offer him my hand, and he hasn't got a lot of choice but to take it. He'd look like a right miserable b. if he didn't.

'All right, Jonny. I'm Chris. Chris Erry. Sorry we got off on the wrong foot.'

I'd always rather be mates than not, so we shake on it and off we go. I expect that someone who's been a fitter as long as Chris will be a fund of stories about the gas business. All the changes in equipment. Problems of technique. The way that sophistication has taken over the industry and ruined the old skills.

I'm partly right.

Chris is a fund of stories all right.

'And then the Irishman says: "How did I know. I thought that it said 'Pull' and so I did". Get it?'

'Yes.'

Not all his stories are about Irishmen. Having exhausted those before we're even halfway towards our first call, Chris moves on to another area.

'So she pulls them up, and I've never seen anything like

it. Talk about big. I'm just poking around when a bloke backs out a big artic and says to me: "Is this the right road for Inverness?" You get it?'

I nod wearily. This is going to be a long and winding apprenticeship. We stop off for a cup of tea and a couple of slices of toast. And wait while Chris plays the machines in the café. By the time he gets ready to leave we are already half an hour late for the first appointment.

'Shouldn't we . . . you know, get going?'

Mister Erry smiles. 'You're young, sonny. Sort of knave, like.'

I guess he means 'naïve'.

'Don't start trying to teach your grandpa to suck eggs, eh?'

Personally, I was never into egg-sucking much as a boy. Nasty and slimy.

'The lady has a note saying we've promised to be there last week. We never made it. Now she thinks we're coming first call today. That's nine. What time do you make it?'

I look at my ticka-tock Timex. 'Ten-fifteen, Chris. And we're still not there.'

'Right. So it'll be at least an hour late. Now, ideally, we should be there this afternoon. Because then she'll be *even* more grateful. Because she'll have totally given up hope, won't she?'

He shakes his head like he's uncovered the secret of eternal life to me and goes on driving the van, throwing it round the corners of North London like he's James Hunt with the World Championship in his grasp.

'Normally, I wouldn't bother going to her at all today. Make them sweat a few weeks and they're so grateful they fall on your neck sobbing.'

Am I going to like this particular job, I am asking myself?

'Did I tell you the one about the Pakki and the blind Jew and the Irishman with the crippled son who all . . .'

'Yes. Yes you did.'

He didn't, but I really don't want to know about it, if you don't mind. I have to get him off this string of terrible jokes. Perhaps if I start telling them myself? No, why waste them on him. I'll save them for you readers. And stop groaning like that or I'll never let you out of the book!

'What about the housewives? Is it like in the ad, with them all trying to get you to have it off?'

'Haw, haw, haw, haw. You're too young for that sort of filth! Want to get the dirty water off your chest, do you? Is that it? See the bleeding bird with the knockers and the frilly knickers and you start creaming your jeans. Don't you?'

He's right, of course, but I'd never admit it. I wonder if I should encourage him to go on.

To try and *stop* him would be like trying to stop a party from Essex Women's Institute getting to the one public lavatory still working after a long, long coach trip.

Why Essex?

I just like the sound of the second part of the word, that's all.

Chris Erry is in full flow.

'Course I'm a married man. Been married for more than twenty years. Haven't had my leg over the old Dutch for the last sixteen. She went . . . I mean that *I* went off it after the birth of our third. Never had it since. I depend on all the spare nookie I can pick up on the job. And there's bleeding plenty of that.'

Nookie is not a word I like. Liz James hates it, and the mere mention of it is enough to ensure you get a boot in the tradesmen's from her. Incidentally, she is still up in Bonny Scotland, having taken the high road to get there. From her last card she seems to be having a good time.

Though I didn't like the sound of 'Hamish who is my tutor. Lang may his wang reek.'

I reckon it sounds like something you read about on those dull notices in public lavs.

'Right scorchers they are, Jonny. Phew. What! I mean, blimey! Rip your trousers off as soon as look at you. Been through more married nookie than you've had hot dinners. Walk in. Ask them where it is, meaning the appliance. And they show you. Just like that. Right out loud. Not so much as wipe your feet. It's drop 'em and shove it. Blimey. I reckon. Hot bleedin' pants they call them and that's what they've got.'

It's verbal diarrhoea. Having pulled out the cork I don't know how to get it back in. Chris raves on like this all the way to the first stop, the veins standing out across his forehead like knots in string, and his eyes popping like mission-hall organ stops. And according to the way he tells it, his organ never stops.

Sweat drips into his moustache and never reappears, which is not a pretty thought.

But at last we're there. A Mrs Brest. Fancy being named after a naval port, I think. And I do know what you're all thinking and you can stop it. Nothing is further from my tits . . . I mean my mind.

She has complained about having a leaky boiler, which can't be a lot of fun. Though come to think of it, and I do, I have had a lot of fun in my day with some very leaky boilers.

We clamber out of the van and I am given the tools to carry.

And I must pause at this point to thank again all the lovely and wicked ladies who have written saying how much they'd like a chance to get their fingers on Jonny's tools. Keep on with that sort of letter in between the jokes and frillies. I love reading them. It's the cold showers afterwards that I hate.

'You keep your young mouth shut, Jonny, and take note of how we experts act.'

Chris knocks on the door, which is opened after about ten seconds by a nice-looking lady in her early thirties. She's not in a transparent dressing-gown and stockings and black knickers, but she is still a nice-looking bit of crackling and I feel the faintest stirrings of interest from Edgar. She smiles, and the Jonny May naughtiness sensor starts clicking. Here is a lady who would not be averse to a bit of the other.

'Morning, Ma'am. I'm Erry.'

'How nice for you to be so happy in your work, whatever that is.'

'No. No, I meant that . . . my name is . . . and we had a message about your boiler and . . . I . . . we . . . that is, my assistant and I . . . thought . . .'

What has happened to old Shove it in Erry? Where has the man of the world gone, and who is this stammering, blushing nit who has replaced him?

Mrs Brest lets us in, and stands in the doorway so that we have to squeeze past her. Chris shuffles along like she's got some frightful Oriental disease, but I am never one to go backward when I can go forward, and I have a good squeeze past, realising that the lady lives up to her name. There are two good reasons for it, but I can't set my tongue to them.

Much as I would like to.

'Where is it, Ma'am?' says Mister Erry, scraping his feet on the carpet like a schoolboy caught by the Chaplain doing that which can make a lad both deaf and blind.

'Where's what?' she asks, with a wealth of meaning that would spring a corpse off the slab. 'Oh, the boiler. That's through there. But I wonder if you'd like to have a look in my bedroom first, Mister . . . Jolly, was it?'

'Merry, Ma'am. I mean, Erry. What's in your bedroom, then?'

'You'd be surprised, you wicked fellow,' she says, laying a hand on his arm. I think for a moment he's going to do an impersonation of a door-lock and bolt.

If I was in his shoes, then I'd have given me a quid and told me to cut and not come back for a couple of hours. Despite all his shooting off at the mouth, Chris doesn't seem as if he is getting her message. I begin to suss out that the mouth might be the only part of Chris that does any shooting off.

'I always seem to have trouble when my husband's away on business. He's in Brussels now. Won't be back for a couple of days.'

By Adult, Ur and Ee! She is laying it on a bit strong. How can he resist?

Easily.

'Well, I don't think we'd . . . I'll just go and look at your boiler.'

'Is that all you *really* want to look at? Isn't it hot in here? I can see you're sweating, Mister Appy.'

'Erry, Ma'am. It is a trifle hot.'

'My bedroom is air-conditioned, Mister Erry. Perhaps your assistant would like to go and have a stroll. Lovely park not far from here.' A thought strikes her. 'Or maybe you'd *both* like to come and enjoy the air-conditioning in the bedroom?'

Group gropes aren't my line. But if old Erry would do a vanishing act, then I reckon that the lady and me could be making the old beast with two backs before you could say 'Clean Brests'.

'We have a job to do, Mrs Brest.'

'Even though it's so hot.' She tugs at her blouse, pulling it down far enough at the front for me to get a good shot of her painted toe-nails.

'The boiler?' says Erry, insisting on doing his job. What devotion to work!

What loyalty to the Gas Board!

What stubborn indifference to the lady's tricks!

What a stupid twat!!!!!

Chris patches up the boiler in no time flat, as though he can't wait to get away from the place. I can't wait to get into the place, but being only an apprentice I don't even get a sniff at the merchandise.

Mrs Brest goes to amazing lengths to interest Erry. She

bangs her leg on a table and pulls her skirt so high that she is in danger of a cold on the tonsils. She wears very short pants, and that is what my breath is coming in.

'Would you like a cup of tea?'

'Yes please,' I say, but old misery-bum says that we mustn't while we're on the job. If I was on the job with Mrs Brest I guess I wouldn't want a drink either.

'Most men feel like something hot when they're working like you are,' says the lady, game to the last, though she must realise by now she's backed a loser.

'Some toast? With marmalade. My husband only likes that feeble stuff with little strips of peel in it.'

'I like it all chunky,' I say, still trying to keep my end up.

'Really. I think that a man is only a true virile man if he likes a bit of danger now and again.'

Personally, I wouldn't call eating chunky marmalade really dangerous. I mean, it's hardly in the North Face of the Eiger league, is it? Then again, I don't know what really goes into it, so maybe I shouldn't talk.

'Personally, I prefer the jelly,' says Mister Erry, sniffing through his moustache. 'The peel gets under me plate if I eat anything else.'

Perhaps Mrs Brest has something in her theory. Try it out on your husband or boy-friend, ladies. Let me know the results of the J. May marmalade survey.

Eventually, we finish the job, and the customer is quite satisfied. Mister Erry thinks she is, but I know a lot better. Before we leave I have a chance to whisper to her: 'Any time you need any more help . . . with your boiler, or anything . . . then ring the Gas Board and ask for Jonny May.'

'You're May?'

'Yes. In fact I won't just may. I promise you I will.'

Christ is loading up the van with his bag of tools. Why he needs such a huge suitcase when he only ever uses a hammer and a screwdriver and a spanner and a bit of sticky tape, is quite beyond me.

'You seem quite a sweet boy,' says Mrs Brest, peering round the door to make sure nobody's watching and giving me a quick once or twice-over on the tool-bag.

'Mmmmm. I hope I get a chance to be of service, Mrs Brest. I'm an up and coming lad.'

She kisses me softly on the lips, still hanging on the equipment. 'I can see you're up, Jonny. And maybe I'll find out later about the second part. Shame my hubbie's back for a few weeks. Next time he goes away, I just wonder if I don't have trouble with my flue.'

Erry reappears looking suspicious, so I don't have to make an answer. Not that I could think of one on the spur of the moment.

'All fixed. I hope you won't need to be seeing us again, Ma'am.'

Mrs Brest favours me with a big wet smile. 'I wouldn't mind seeing quite a lot more of you, Mister May.'

We walk off down the front path and climb into the van. She is still stood standing in the doorway, and gives me a wave. I wave back, feeling my trousers gradually returning to their normal not quite so tight state.

Mister Erry crashes his way through the gears and we drive off in silence. But after four or five minutes he recovers all of his old self-confidence and starts telling awful so-called jokes about African lepers and Irish deaf-mutes.

We pull into a transport café and he stops. Turns in his seat and grins at me. 'That Mrs Brest.'

'Nice lady, I thought.'

'Yeah.' A soggy tongue flicks at the even soggier corners of his moustache. 'Know what I think about her? If I'd played my cards right, I reckon she could have been screwed. Yeah, that lady actually could have been screwed!'

Chapter Nine

Actually, during the couple of weeks that I work with merry Erry, he shows me a side of himself that makes it easier to understand why he didn't take up Mrs Brest on her obvious offers. And she is not alone. It's true what Chris says about the housewives of England. A surprising number of them will do a turn for anyone from a milkman to a window-cleaner, with gasmen well to the front.

Not many of them seem worried by the fact that there were two of us, either. I haven't seen so much of the nudge-nudge since the last lamented series of Mister Python and his aerial entertainment. But with Mister Erry along, they are safe as if they were locked away in a convent with only bread and water to eat and only candles.

Only candles for lighting!!!

Same old thing, wick in and wick out.

One day I'm sitting in the van with Chris Erry, and he starts talking about married nookie. By now I've sussed out that he's all talk. Yet he still makes the jokes about the way women will drop their knickers for a gasman but in nearly a fortnight all I've seen is him making excuses and backing away quicker than a cowardly toreador. Not that I blame such men. I wouldn't fancy being attacked by fifteen hundred pounds of angry rissole on the hoof.

Gore blimey!

'You've probably had it off loads of times, what with all this permissive society and all that?'

'I've done all right,' I reply modestly.

'Yeah. I'm always getting offered it. Seen that for yourself, haven't you?'

'Yes. Seen it being offered, Chris.'

'Well. Got more than I can handle.'

'Yeah.'

'Jonny. I mean, you've had it a lot. With lots of different birds. Quite often. Had it away. Haven't you?'

'That's right, Chris. Why?'

'Well. I just wondered.'

'What.'

'What's it like, Jonny?'

Sad, really.

The two weeks with Mister Erry drift by. Nothing very exciting happens. I see Mandy Ranndee a couple of times, and hear about her work. And that of Polly Inger.

Seems that Mandy is not the brightest thing on two legs. The fitter who has her keeps complaining about her, saying that he has to tell her everything. Even if he asks her something for a joke, she still goes and does it. Like trying to find a left-handed screw-driver and some nails with points on the other end for the far side of some casing.

'I'd love to have her working under me, in one way,' I hear him saying in the canteen. 'But in the other way, she's bleeding death. I've never seen anyone so accident-prone in all my life. Yesterday I've got this thin tubing laid all along a wall. Taken me bleeding hours. Then I find it's a bit short. So I say to her that I wish I had a foot on the end. Next thing I know the silly bitch's trodden on it.'

Not that my old mum's a lot better in things like that. I

remember the time that Morrie is living away from home for the first time. He writes back saying that because of having good food for the first time in his life, he's grown another foot.

So my old mum promptly knits him an extra sock.

I pass the first couple of weeks with no trouble. I hear from our boss that Polly and I are their two top pupils, and he hints that there may be some sort of reward in the wind for us. As long as it's crisp and folding with a picture of the Queen on it I won't mind.

I'm finding myself in a better financial position than for a long time. I am able to buy a couple of new albums – Waylon Jennings and Don Williams, actually – and a new pair of jeans. Plus a cord shirt as the nights are getting colder. Which is what happened when the Crusaders fought their way east in winter. The knights got colder.

In days of old,
When knights were bold,
And suits were made of tin,
They had to use tin-openers,
To get them out and in.

That's from 'Some of my Worse' by Jonathan May. A new collection of poems out soon. As far as I'm concerned, you can never have it out too soon.

Too late, yes. Too soon, no.

Liz sends me another card showing a big fat Scot heaving this huge chunk of wood around the place. It's called 'Tossing the Caber'. Or 'Chucking the Chipboard' or 'Toting the Pole'. Her card says that I'd be amazed at the muscles that this exercise builds up. Since I have no wish to be the most perfectly ruptured man in Britain, I take no notice.

She seems to be getting on well up there, and mentions how nice she is finding it working under Hamish. I don't like the sound of it, folks. Still, I suppose she'll be able to tell me what they really do wear underneath the kilt.

My Aunt Rose once has a very nasty experience with a Scottish football supporter. I know you think most Scottish supporters are called 'Jock Strap', but they're not.

This one, whose name happened to be Ben Down, and who is the cousin of Phil McCavity, is in Birmingham to cheer on one of those football teams from Glasgow. Can't remember which one it is.

He meets Aunt Rose, who hangs around pubs when there's visiting supporters, in the hope of a quick fiver. As you don't know Aunt Rose I should explain that the fiver refers to five pence, that being all her particular market will stand.

Actually, she's not that ugly. She just wears the mask to stop the dogs howling.

Aunt Rose meets this Ben Down, and before you can say: 'Fancy a nice time, dearie?' they're off back to her rooms. They get into bed and the Scot tells her that he can only do it with the light off, so Aunt Rose turns off the light. She doesn't care either way, and I'm not just talking about the light.

They have it off, and Ben Down says he has to go for a pee, so he slopes off into the bathroom next door.

Just as Aunt Rose is starting to get up, the door opens and in comes the McCasanova. Jumps on the bed, the light's still off, and away they go again.

As soon as they've finished, he leaps up, muttering something in his hairy language about the toilet, and vanishes next door.

Just as Aunt Rose is about to get up and put the light on, the door opens, and in . . .

And so on . . .

And so on.

After the eighteenth time, Aunt Rose is beginning to get a wee bit sore. Or is it her wee bit that's getting sore? And she reckons that Ben Down is having rather more than his money's worth.

So before he comes back from the bathroom, she nips out on the landing. Nothing there. Back in bed just in time to hear someone else climbing into bed.

She puts on the light and . . . it's a total stranger.

'What are you doing here?' she screams.

The bloke looks puzzled. 'Don't ask me, darling. Ask that big Scotsman selling tickets downstairs!'

At last I'm off on my own. A fully qualified gas fitter, ready to battle with the forces of leaks and stoppages, and prepared to undertake conversions. The only thing I don't do is exorcisms, so you can stop turning your head round and throwing up green emulsion.

I have my own little van, which has a gearbox that feels as it's made out of Lego. In fact, I reckon that a gearbox made out of Lego would probably go better than this one does.

I have a walkie-talkie radio so that I can be sent speeding to where the action is. It's great. Just like on the telly.

'Negatory Big Daddy. There is a bear in the air blocking the A248 and then the gate is open clear through to Potters Bar. This is the Confessor in the Gas buggy, come on.'

Not really like that, but you can dream.

Actually, the messages go something like this.

'Jonny. Oh, bugger! The bleeding . . . Jonny are . . . Over and through the . . . Longhurst Road at . . . fridge . . . Sod it . . . All right?'

Funnily enough, my first call that I actually get to hear is for a snobby block of flats not far from where I live in Notting Hill. Delacourt Mansions. Sort of place where they have a porter in the front hall who looks at you like you might be something smuggled in on a banana boat from Bangladesh or a cheap day return from Calais.

It's much like any other block of high-rise flats that you and I know well. Only there's not a lot of noise in the corridors, which have carpets anyway. No slogans on the walls. No

'Jonny May rules O.K.'. No broken light bulbs on the stairs. No sick stains in the corners. No turds in the lifts, which work, anyway.

Like I say. Just the same as any other block of flats that we knew. Money might not buy you happiness but it makes a lot of difference to where you can live.

I pass by little Adolf on the door, who rings up to the customer to make sure I'm not a master criminal about to sneak out in a mask with a big bag labelled 'Swag'. I know he's only doing his job, but he doesn't have to be such a suspicious and miserable so-and-so.

'Wipe your shoes, sonny,' he calls out after me as I make for the lift.

'Bring your tongue over here, then,' I reply with the bright wit that has made me the scourge of traffic wardens from Notting Hill to Queensway.

I am glad to say that the lift arrives at that moment as the porter is laying down his copy of *Body-Builder and Boxing Life* with a certain menace.

As my Uncle Nick is always telling me. He who doesn't fight but runs away, lives to run away another day.

The flat is number 69. What a surprise. Do you realise that the number is the same upside-down. Just like when you do it. Could it be that's why it's called 'Sixty-Nine'?

(Publisher's Note: Haven't heard from me for some time, so I thought I'd just sort of slip in for a second to let you know I'm still here.)

By Ah and Soul! How that man gives himself away about his own performance in bed. The word 'slip' and 'for a second'. It's uncanny the way it all ties in with what his wife says.

And I won't tell you about why I laugh when his secretary tells me that he's 'tied up at the moment'.

It's all those James Bondage books he reads.

The doorbell chimes some bit of classical music. You intellectuals out there probably know it. It goes 'breasts, buttocks, breasts, buttocks, breasts, buttocks, buttocks, buttocks'.

(Publisher's Note: What?)

Make it easier. 'Titty, bum, titty, bum, titty, bum, bum, bum'.

William Tell Overture.

The lady who opens the door talks just like that snooty neighbour in that telly programme 'The Good Life'. Penelope Keith her name is. Great. This bird is shorter, and a bit younger, but the voice is spot-on the same.

'Mrs Prendergastly?'

'Miss, actually. I'm separated from my so-called husband who used to spend most of his time in bed with me talking about the young boys he knew when he lived in Greece.'

By Inn, Disc and Reet! If she talks like this to me I wonder what her analyst hears.

'I'm Jonathan May and I have come from the Gas Board to check your supply.'

Do I imagine it, or does one of those well-plucked eyebrows raise an inch or two?

'Can I see your credentials?'

There it goes again. Not more than a sixteenth of an inch, but a definite movement.

'Hang on while I open my zip and pull them out for you.'

Well, two can play at the game of doubling entendres. Just so long as they're not mixed doubles.

I show her my identification cards which she peruses like she's either very suspicious or she normally wears glasses and is too vain to put them on.

'Very well, come in. I suppose you'll want to start poking around everywhere with your little tools?'

There it goes again. This time it was the eyebrow *and* a slight stress on the word 'everywhere'.

'Yes. But not all of my tools are that small, Miss Prendergastly. Some of the ladies I've been to service have been quite surprised at the size of them.'

'Really. Pleasantly surprised, I hope.'

'Oh, yes. I haven't had a single complaint.'

'Yet.'

And that puts yours very truly well into his place.

Miss Prendergastly swings along through the hall, into the kitchen pointing out to me where the meter is and the oven and fridge. The oven looks like something out of Star Trek, with all sorts of dials and clocks that enable you to cook badly and also pay more for the privilege. My old mum would have a field day with a cooker like this. Not only can she cook badly, but she can get the timing wrong as well.

I sit on the floor and start unpacking my tools, while the lady of the house . . . sorry, flat . . . sits on the stripped pine work surface, her legs swinging. Trying not to make it obvious that I'm looking, I eye high up her thighs. A thigh-high eye for I. Nice legs. It's warm inside – the flat I mean – and she isn't wearing either tights (yeukk) or stockings (shame).

Very good legs indeed. I am so low down on the floor that I can see a tempting vee of white at the veeeeeeeeery top of her legs.

'Do you normally work in that position?'

'Oooh. Er, no. I was just weighing up the situation and trying to decide what the best course of action is.'

'The best and quickest way between two points is a straight line, I was always told at my finishing school.'

She crosses her legs. White lace, I notice, around the tops of the thighs.

'Do you wish to use the loo?'

'No thanks. Why?'

'You look a little flushed.'

And she gives a tinkling laugh and swings down off the seat and vanishes into one of the other rooms. After the tinkling laugh I hear the tinkling of ice in glass, and I wonder if the freeby booze is going to flow my way.

'Would you like a drinkie?'

'Yes, please.' I was right. Miss Prendergastly is going to turn into a cracker.

'There's water in the tap.'

One of those crackers that go 'pfffffť' instead of 'BANG!!'

I get on with my work, and I can hear her in the other room, walking around and singing to herself. There is also the frequent noise of liquid being poured into a glass and the gurgling of it being downed in one.

There is a bit of routine maintenance, but the main request was for me to have a look at the water heater in the bathroom.

'Fuming,' was the message I got. But I'm not sure if it refers to the heater or to Miss Prendergastly.

'Where's the bathroom?' I shout.

'Couldn't you have gone before you came?' replies the cool and witty lady.

It's funny, but she's being very rude and distant with me, yet there's something going on between us that I can't quite figure. All I need is a clue as to what she wants, and Jonny will be there.

I find my way to the bathroom, which is covered with the most fantastic carpet I've ever seen. It's knee-high, and soft and white. There's a white bog and a white bath with gold taps and a white wash-basin. Also one of those white foot-washing things that aren't for washing your feet.

(Publisher's Note: Mister May clearly does not recognise a bidet. He has no skill with his tongue.)

I hate to have to mention it, but that's what his wife says about him.

Just as I'm sitting down under the heater, trying to guess what's wrong with it, in comes Miss Prendergastly. I don't know what she's been drinking, but I can make a reasonable guess at how much. Something between a bottle and five bottles by the sloppy grin. She pats me on the head as she staggers past and sits down on the crapper.

For a moment I wonder if she intends to . . . but it seems just to be a convenient seat. A private convenience. Uncle Nick once works in a public lavatory and the council ask him to collect his wages from their head office, but he asks if he can be paid at his convenience.

'Will you be very long, Jonathan?'

'About the usual length.'

'And what is that?'

'A secret between my conscience and the ballot-box,' I reply.

She sits there, swinging her long legs, smiling at me. I notice that the more she swings, the more I can see. Those beautiful thighs, ending in the white vee of . . . Just a gosh-darned minute!

I'll be hornswoggled if she hasn't changed her undies. Must be expecting a road-accident. You never know. I've often had to pull out to avoid a child.

Now she seems . . . I stare harder . . . to be wearing a pair of fur frillies. I can see so fur and no farther.

'Like what you can see, Jonathan?' asks Miss Prendergastly, standing up and wading through the carpet to stand right alongside me.

'Yes. But I'm here really to do something to your thing in the bathroom.'

She sits down by me, hoicking her skirt up round her waist, which must result in the carpet tickling her fancy. And puts an elegant arm across my shoulders.

'Well, I'm in the bathroom. You're in the bathroom. And I can promise you that my thing is also in the bathroom.'

'But it's the heating!' I say weakly, as her hand has wriggled around my neck and under the collar of my shirt and is playing 'Deep in the heart of Texas' on my left press-stud.

'Yes. I'd like to see your central heating, Jonathan. The customer is always tight, remember.'

She said it, not me.

I can't believe that this isn't all happening in a film. This rich bird is lying back, almost disappearing into the pile of the white furry carpet. Arms open wide like a certain goal-keeper when he's just misjudged a near-post cross. Legs open wide like someone demonstrating the action of the breast-stroke leg-kick. Which is a whole lot more comfortable than the leg-stroke breast-kick.

'Miss Prendergastly. What do you really want from me?'

'Can't you guess?'

The skirt is tugged up right over her waist and I can see the fur panties. They're so cleverly designed that it almost looks as if she's not wearing . . .

Any . . .

At . . .

All . . .

The mutton machete gets plenty of exercise from Miss Prendergastly. I don't know whether she goes riding a lot, but I am grateful for the soft carpet under my shoulders as she goes for a swift gallop. Edgar begins to feel like something out of the Boat Race with all this in and out and in and out. One minute he's freezing in the basement and the next second he's banging his head on the ceiling.

And I do mean banging.

I suss out that the lady is one of those rich, bored bints who go in for lorry drivers. And gasmen. Bit of the rough trade. Some people don't like that, feeling that the birds are using them. But Jonny May is all for equality – within reason – and I don't mind being used like that. I get a lot of pleasure out of her, and Miss Prendergastly indicates in the most subtle manner that she is enjoying thingies.

'Yeeeeeeeeeeeeeeeeeeeeeeeeeeeeeeeeeeeeeeees!!!!!'

That's first time.

She's very athletic and the second time, with me in the saddle this turn around, leaves us in a very complicated position. I've read the Calmer Suitor and I don't remember it in there.

It's all a bit hazy, but I have my left leg wrapped round the foot-washer, and my right leg hooked over the side of the bath. If I move it a couple of inches I can probably go tap-dancing.

One arm is over and one arm under, with my ten troopers invading friendly territory. Miss Prendergastly has both legs in between mine, but one is hooked up and between, making me feel a bit of a heel. One of her arms is hanging on the wash-basin to give a bit of purchase, while the other is wrapped around my shoulders.

Our lips are in close contact in a tooth-to-tooth situation. Which results in a nice bit of pressed tongue. I am glad that I lead a clean healthy life, as what we are doing would wreck the prospects of anyone whose body was not a superb instrument, honed to perfection.

After we've squeezed through the turnstile together, we unwrap ourselves from the bathroom furniture. Sticky business this thingie. Although having it away on a big deep rug has its advantages, there are also disadvantages, as I find out when I try to get up.

Still, my old man always encouraged me to get stuck into my work.

Miss Prendergastly sees my predicament and crawls over to help, suggesting that we both have a shower. This is very pleasant and I find having my back scrubbed helps me to relax. When she starts to rub my front, I sense that my spirits are rising.

But I still say that it would have been all right if she hadn't dropped the soap and bent over to pick it up. Edgar sees his chance and is in faster than a hot knife through butter. He feels a little lovelier each day, does Edgar. And the lovely he feels obviously enjoys herself.

After it's all over I get dressed, while Miss Prendergastly throws on her skirt and top. I notice that the white panties have reappeared. And then disappeared.

'Thank you very much, Jonathan,' says the bird, as calm as if I've just laid the table and not her. 'I shall be in touch with your employers to recommend your hard work. Such an attitude is rare these days.'

The attitude we finished up in on the floor is very rare these days. In fact I doubt if anyone's heard of it before.

All in a day's work, it is. And she was a lovely lay. Real class there. You can tell. It's the way she sounds her aitches when she screams: 'Hold on and don't hurry!!!'

So my first customer is extremely satisfied.

I wonder how long it takes her to realise that I never got round to mending her heater after all.

Quickie to finish a naughty chapter.

What's big and hairy and sticks out of your pyjamas?

Your head.

Chapter Ten

I'm sitting back in the offices at the Gas place waiting for a meeting with one of the bosses. And to stop you jumping to any conclusions I will say right out that I have not dropped any bullocks around the place and am not in the dog house. This job is a breeze. Good pay. Travel. Meet lots of interesting people. Couldn't ask for more. Sounds like an ad for gas fitters, doesn't it?

Actually, the reason that I am sitting here is that we have all been called in for a special chat. By 'all' I mean those of us who joined up at the same time. Including Miss Inger and Mandy Ranndee.

Polly has put the kettle on and we are all going to have tea.

She is so efficient this girl. She's up in the morning, out on the job, works like the devil for her pay. While that lucky old sun ain't got nothing . . . Sorry.

Shame she is not the most attractive thing on two legs. If she had Mandy's looks and her own brains, she'd be the next Prime Minister, not that I'd wish a job like that on a dead dog.

Mandy is perched up on top of one of the filing cabinets. You can tell how bright she is by the fact that she is using the filing cabinet to file her nails.

I hear from one of the girls in the office that Miss Ranndee didn't make the bosses any happier with her strange system of classifying correspondence and dockets.

She was asked to produce orders from a Mister Aardvark, a Mister Queenly and a Mister Zzyxx. The office manager was a bit befuddled when she goes to the filing drawer marked 'M' and starts looking through great sheafs of letters and bills and orders.

'Miss Ranndee?' he says.

'Yes?'

'Why are you searching for Mister Aardvark, Mister Queenly and Mister Zzyxx under the letter "M".'

'It's obvious, innit?' she chirps brightly through a mouth filled with chewing-gum. 'They all go under "M" for "Mister".'

Seeing her sitting up there is not doing me a lot of good, with the lead filling my pencil. And if she opens her legs any wider her pencil-sharpener is going to catch cold and die of exposure.

I try to think about something else while I wait for the boss. And I remember a joke that I must pass on to you.

There's this emergent African State busily emerging, and they've sent observers to all the European countries to make sure they set up a system of government based on all that's best in the West.

They greatly admire the British methods of law, and they establish their own court in their capital, based on the Old Bailey. The same in every detail. Clothes of judges. The placing of the witness box. The lot.

After they've been running for a couple of months they ask over one of Britain's top criminal lawyers, who's had more briefs than a Soho stripper. Just to come and see how they're doing and to give them any advice.

He arrives and spends a couple of days in the court, just

as an observer. He'd rather be a sunday times, but can't manage it.

He's very impressed by everything. It's just like being back home. Uncanny the way they've done the whole works so precisely like Britain.

Apart from one thing.

Every now and then, for no reason that he can suss out, this pigmy runs into court, wearing only a loincloth, and carrying a blow pipe, scampering around while nobody takes a blind bit of notice of him.

The little native goes up to every woman in the court and squeezes each of them on the boobs. The shorthand writers. Couple of ladies in the jury box. Several women up in the public gallery. Then runs out again.

This happens half a dozen times during the day. Exactly the same. Pigmy comes in, and touches up all the birds on their Bristols, and goes out again.

That night the English barrister is dining with his host, who is one of the judges. And he gets asked what he thinks of their legal operation.

'Very good. Most impressed.'

'Excellent,' beams his host, who passes him a fine old port. Coburns, I believe. Pronounced 'Cock'. 'We obtained all of our information from reading reports in English papers of what happens in trials.'

'Only one thing puzzled me,' says the Englishman.

'What is that?'

'The very small man who ran round and touched all of the ladies in the court-room on their bosom. I didn't understand that.'

'Ah, ha,' says the African. 'As I tell you, we read all about things in papers and magazines, and we are determined that all will be just as in England.'

'So?'

'So, we always read in such papers that every now and then a small titter runs round court.'

Please yourself.

It passes a bit of time while we all wait for the Mister Big, who finally appears ten minutes late bringing in with him the pleasant aroma of business efficiency and gin.

'Right gentlemen,' he begins. 'And ladies, of course,' seeing Polly beaming brightly and Mandy clambering down off the filing cabinet revealing a great deal of her main assets.

We all shuffle and cough the way you do when someone comes in to chat to you. There's an extinguishing of fags from those who use the unpleasant weed, and a careful easing of gussets all round.

Mister Big . . . that isn't really his name, of course. His real name, surprisingly, is Mister Weeny. Mister Weeny raps on the table for a bit of hush.

'Ladies and gentlemen. I have some wonderful news for you all.'

My brother Morrie's been arrested!

No, of course. He wouldn't possibly know my brother Morrie. The black wolf of the family. The only greater shame my family ever suffered was when I joined the police force a few months ago.

(Publi . . .

I know! I'm going to. *Confessions From The Beat* is the name of the book. Packed with knicker-nicking and other amazing incidents. Makes the Sweeney look like Dixon of Dock Green.

'There is going to be a demonstration.'

'Against canteen tea?'

He favours me with the sort of look that the Rolling Stones give the Bay City Rollers. Or, if you prefer it, that a West Bromwich Albion supporter give a Chelsea supporter.

'Mister May . . . If I may proceed with what I was going to say before your crass interruption.'

'Sorry. I can never keep off the crass.'

'Mister May!!'

'Sorry.'

'We have been the victims of some rather unfavourable and chilling exposure.'

'Why don't we buy some nice warm woollen combs, then, Mister Weeny?'

His eyes narrow like Lee Van Cleef. Sadly Mister Weeny is only five feet tall and weighs a good eighteen stone, so there the resemblance ends.

'Mister May. This is my last warning. Interrupt me again and only one of us will remain in this room.'

'Please don't leave on my account, Mister Weeny,' I say politely.

'Not me, you blithering idiot. You. You Mister May.'

'That's right. Me Mister May and you Mister Weeny.'

Perhaps the poor man is having a brainstorm. I wonder if I should loosen his collar which seems to be vanishing into rolls of purple fat.

'I . . . I . . . I don't think that I can go on like this. I can't.'

'Perhaps if you lose some weight, you might feel better. My Uncle Angus . . .'

'I don't want to know about your damned Uncle Angus!'

'That's good, because I just remembered that it's Aunt Rose I was going to tell you about. Being overweight and all that.'

'NO!'

'Really. She was. People said that my Aunt Rose didn't just keep her girlish figure. She actually managed to double it.'

With a massive effort, my boss manages to control himself. He grips the edge of the table like he's doing some of those funny American exercises for tired businessmen. He closes his eyes and breathes deeply, and I'm sure I hear him whisper to the table-top: 'No jury on earth would convict,' but maybe I mishear, as that doesn't make sense.

'One last time, Mister May, I shall try and say what I have come here to say, and if you so much as open your mouth I shall have you instantly dismissed. You will not open your mouth.'

I nod wisely and begin to breathe very noisily through my nose.

He goes on. 'There have been some unfavourable reports in the Press mentioning a series of unfortunate accidents involving the installation of new apparatus and equipment. Frankly, the public are beginning to lose confidence in us.'

I wonder why that is.

'So the powers that be,' he says, pointing vaguely in the direction of the ceiling in such a reverential manner that I wonder if he means the Celestial overlords with their gas-powered harps.

'The powers that be have decided that we will stage a demo for the benefit of the press. Two fitters, both among our most recent intake, and one of them not of the male gender.' He pauses and laughs the laugh that he practised last night in his wardrobe mirror. It doesn't look any better to us than it did last night to him.

'Have to pick my words carefully since the Sex Discrimination nonsense came around. Not that I ever found it hard to discriminate between the sexes.'

He is so short and fat that I bet he hasn't found a woman who would stomach him.

'So it means that one of you two ladies, and one of you lads, will be representing the honour of the Gas Board in this demo, fourteen days from now. It'll only be a simple job, connecting up some pipes so that each member of the Press has a small gas jet in front of him . . . or her . . . that will light up at the right moment.'

I am enthused by an enormous wave of apathy.

'This could be a very big break.'

Like having your leg trodden on by an elephant.

'It will help the Gas Board.'

Who are normally good at helping themselves.

'And there's a fat bonus for the couple that are picked for the demonstration.'

He is nearly trampled in the rush, led by me.

'Wait.'

We wait.

'It's not a question of wanting volunteers. There is the matter of presenting a favourable image to the gentlemen of the Press.'

Is it my imagination or does the miserable old toe-rag stare at me when he says that?

'Are there any questions?'

I put up my hand, being never very backwards at coming forwards when the reward for coming forwards is not going to send me backwards.

'Yes, Mister May?'

'Yes, Mister Weeny, sir. I wonder, sir, if you would be kind enough to explain to us all in that marvellously clear and concise way of yours, sir, exactly how the lucky people are going to be selected for this very great honour, sir.' I throw in an extra 'sir' for good measure. I believe in giving good measure for measure.

I also believe that a little flattery goes a long way. I am right. Mister Weeny actually smiles at me, ignoring the low cries of : 'Creeper' and 'Crawler' and 'Toady' that ring around the room from my envious fellows.

'Good question, Mister May. Glad to see you're controlling your youthful exuberance.'

So soon he forgets.

'I encourage this sort of debate.'

And you know what 'debate' is, don't you? It's what lures de fish.

Sorry about that. Shouldn't have interrupted that wonderfully warm and vibrant human being. Old Blue Meeny.

'We already have progress reports on your work so far, and they make mixed reading.'

That means they're not suitable for reading in mixed company.

'There are only five of you who seem to measure up to what we want and those five will be notified privately and will be asked to sit a simple extra test this afternoon. Any more questions.'

'How much?'

'Well, Miss Ranndee,' and that shows you lot who thought it must be Jonny asking. 'We think an extra bonus in the region of one hundred pounds.'

Holy broken U-Joints, Gasman! Better than a quick jab with the sharp end. I could buy some more sounds. Pair of jeans. Even have a little something ready for the lovely Liz James when she returns from Scotland. That's apart from the big something that is always ready for her.

I'm in.

So's Polly, and so's Mandy. Obviously the former should be, as her record is more impeccable than Cliff Richard. But what about Miss Ranndee?

Unless I miss my guess, the flying fickle finger of bribery has been tickling around these parts. Or, to be more accurate, her parts.

I am passing by Mister Weeny's office after a quick bite on a cupcake in the canteen when I hear noises that sound rather like Mister Weeny is also having a nibble on a cupcake or two. Not more than two. Mandy is a big girl but not that big. And I hear a voice that sounds like her mumbling as though she has her mouth full about how she'll never forget this.

So, it is no surprise to see the usually dense Miss Ranndee scribbling away like a demented traffic warden during the exam. I am sitting right behind her and I notice that she has a strange skin condition on her left wrist, which involves her rolling up the sleeve of her blouse and staring intently at some faint blue marks that have appeared there. Marks that are oddly missing after the exam is over.

I won't bore you with any more examples of the high level of brain-power expected from men such as I, but you'll remember the entrance examination I pass with flying colours. Normally the only thing that anyone in the May family passes is wind.

But Mandy is obviously still doing exactly what she's told, and wins by a short head from Polly Inger. She breasts the line a couple of inches in front of Polly, which is a bit unfair as she has a lot more than a couple of inches in hand in the breasting area. And I would love to get a few inches of her breasting area in hand.

The Lord said 'Come forth and win my love.'

Jonny May comes third and wins a chance to get his fingers on one hundred crispy oncers.

The rest nowhere.

As we file out, Mister Weeny asks Miss Ranndee and myself to remain behind for further briefing. Mandy has to slip off to the loo, all overcome with the excitement, and the Boss and I are left alone. Jonny is not one to shirk saying what he thinks. Not now he's got the place for the demo.

'You fiddled it with Mandy, didn't you?'

He turns whiter than a detergent ad. 'I never fiddled with her at all.'

I know he's all bluster. It's bluster's last stand.

'In your office. Making sure that her credentials were in order.'

'Well, Jonny, you're a man of the world, aren't you?'

I nod my head, looking man of the wordly. Last time I practise this in front of a mirror it doesn't impress me, seeming to look not very man of worldly and rather more like a man with a coke bottle stuck up his bum. However, Weeny is past noticing little details like that.

'Problem is about the girl who really won.'

'Polly?'

'Miss Inger, yes. Trouble is she's . . . how shall I put it?'

'Perhaps you'd rather not put it as far as Polly is concerned? Is that it?'

'Yes. Precisely. Exactly. Spot on. Right. Correct.'

'You mean I've hit the nail on the head.'

'That's what I mean, Jonny. I can see we're getting on like a . . . '

'House on fire?'

'Yes. Situation like this and it's vital that we both remain . . . '

'Cool as cucumbers?'

'Yes. I mean, I bet you haven't played all the games by all the rules. Eh? Nod's as good as a . . . '

'A wink?'

'Yes. People in . . . '

'Glass houses?'

'Shouldn't . . . '

'Throw stones.'

'Let the dust settle. Let . . . '

'Sleeping dogs lie?'

Weeny thinks that he and I are getting on like . . . Oh, I've done that one.

'I'll keep my mouth shut about it.'

'Good lad, Jonny.'

'For another fifty pounds.'

'Fifty pounds!'

'Did I say that? I meant an extra hundred pounds.'

'Hundred pounds!!!'

'Slip of the tongue. I meant first off to ask you for the phone number of the *News Of The World* and second I meant to say I'd keep my mouth closed about you having it off with Mandy and cheating for the telly just because Polly isn't Raquel Welch. In fact she isn't even Leslie Welch, the Memory man. So it's one hundred and fifty pounds.'

'It's a deal.'

'Good, Mister Meeny. As easy as . . .'

'Falling off a log, May. Falling right off a bleeding log!!'

And so it is.

Mister Weeny makes the official announcement that Jonathan May and Miss Mandy Ranndee have been selected for the great honour of representing the Board at this telly and press demo. At the moment the honour is on. Honour off, I don't mind.

We get the congratulations from our sporting fellows, one of whom takes the chance to slip a mouldy doughnut in my jacket pocket. No doubt it was well meant.

As is my reciprocal gesture of squirting an aerosol can of fly killer through the keyhole of his locker. Scented fly killer. And his clothes are in the locker at the time.

So we have a fortnight to train, while we carry on with our normal duties during mornings only. Mandy Ranndee gives me a wet kiss on the cheek and gushes how pleased she is we're going to be working together.

But I have doubts as to whether Polly Inger might not be a better bet in the situation. The demo is very important and if we make a boob, and with Mandy's figure that's not at all impossible, then we are going to be out of a job. I know I can rely on Polly not to cock it up on the job. All I know about

Mandy is that there is bound to be at least one cock up while we are on the job. No prizes for guessing whose.

Still, the idea of appearing on telly is attractive, as I have always cherished a secret feeling . . . not that one . . . that I might be an undiscovered talent that would make hearts throb all over England. If I play my cards right, and don't end up with the joker, I could be all over the newspapers.

My family would at last be proud of me instead of having to pretend that I don't exist. Jonny May – Superstar! It has a nicer ring than Bravingtons.

Funnily enough, my sister Melanie once tries to make it in the movies, and ends up getting made. She has a screen test that begins in the producer's office and finishes up in the same place.

When she walks in he looks her up and down, while stroking his chin. Ten seconds later he's rubbing her up and down while stroking . . . well, this is family reading.

But he asks her to come and sit on his lap, and then asks her if she wants to be a star.

Melanie wriggles around a lot and giggles and plays with his tie.

'I don't really know. Do you think that I could become a star?'

He bounces her up and down and round and round on his lap for a few seconds before answering.

'I guess so, little lady. As far as I'm concerned, you're already starting to make it big.'

Chapter Eleven

The luck of the Brummies is still with me. Those of you who have battled loyally with me through all of my other adventures will be aware that the luck of the Brummies is not necessarily bad luck at all. Just a sort of sloppy good luck.

Generally culminating in total disaster.

But even with the lovely and brainless Miss Ranndee, I don't see that anything too serious can go wrong.

I know it's a demonstration of installing gas equipment, but gas is really a very safe thing. As long as you don't do anything that is really blindingly stupid, like looking for a leak with a naked light.

A naked bird, yes. But not a naked light.

Incidentally, before I pass on to tell you a strange incident that happens to me in the week immediately before the demonstration, I must again tell you a very short truth about Brummies to convince you that jokes about the Irish are as nothing compared with jokes about Brummies.

Do you know that it takes three Brummies to rape one woman? It does. One to actually do it. One to hold the torch. And the third one to read the instructions!

This job is one of the best I've ever had. I like the freedom you get, as well as the bread that you pick up. Despite the rank taxes, which make a change from the taxi rank, there is still enough left over after everything for me to put a bit away each week for Liz in the plaster model of Max Bygraves that I bought to replace the one I broke a book or two ago.

Sort of Save-alonga-Max.

I reckon that if nothing goes wrong with things in the next two or three weeks, then I'm made. The bosses are very pleased with me. Mister Meeny is specially pleased with the way that I have kept both my promise *and* my mouth shut about knowing he and Mandy were busy in his office that lunch hour when both of them had their mouths filled with something that wasn't old Colonel What'sisname's chicken cheapo special.

So, promotion beckons. If I was a German footballer it would be beckonbauer.

I must keep my nose clean. That's what has frustrated me in every job I've ever had. Dirty nostrils. No!! Actually it's that the fates always seem to trip me up at the last moment just when the prize is within my grasp.

Speaking of which subject, I have to admit that Jonny has been doing a fair bit of grasping in the last couple of weeks. Once you suss out the technical side of the job, it's all pretty straight, not to mention forward. So there's often a bit of time to spare. Or, to put it another way, and I love it when a lady puts it another way, there is also time for a bit of the old spare.

I never tire of spare.

And one of the most surprising things about being a gasman is that you are always in and out of married ladies' front doors. And that is not all of married ladies that Jonny is in and out of.

The moment they open the door with wide eyes and say: 'Ooh, thank goodness you've come. I've been waiting in for you.' Then you know that you've cracked it.

Husbands throughout the land would be horrified if they knew just how often their ripe little peaches were getting plucked while they were slaving away at the office trying to get the secretary to work better by screwing her to the desk.

Funny how one thought leads to another. I remember once going with Uncle Angus to a football match up at the Hawthorns in West Bromwich. They were playing those candidates for comedy outfit of the year, and I won't upset any Chelsea supporters by mentioning their team.

Did I?

Sorry. So I did.

Uncle Angus has got some season tickets and I sit next to him, with Aunt Rose the other end.

To my amazement, before the match starts, there's a steady procession of men coming up to Aunt Rose. First one gropes her legs. Next one kisses her on the mouth. Third one shoves his hand down the bra. Fourth one rams an arm up her skirt. And she responds by kissing them, and touching them up. Right in front of everyone, including Uncle Angus.

After this has been going on for twenty minutes, I can stand it no longer. Can you stand it longer, Missus?

I turn to my Uncle and say: 'How on earth can you let her get away with this behaviour? Why did you bring her?'

He shakes his head sorrowfully and replies: 'Had to. If I leave her at home she sleeps with everyone!'

That reminds me of another football tale about a famous player. The best, they say. But I'll save it. Maybe tell it you later if you're all good.

By an amazing coincidence, the job that I was talking about happens to be not all that far from the Chelsea ground. Or the 'bargain basement' as it's known in certain areas. But I guess that the young lady who opens the door of this smart house is not a Chelsea supporter. I can tell as she looks quite normal.

By the way she talks I guess that she is more likely to be the sort of bird who spends her Saturdays going to Twickers with Rodders in the Jaggers and then going for drinkers at a super little pub near Kew and then going to bedders.

And often getting preggers as well.

Then getting marrieders.

And divorcers.

And alcoholicers.

But all this is in the future. She is a pretty girl of about eighteen, wearing the outfit of the Sloane Rangers, named after Sloane Square where so many of them live and/or work. She's got a sensible two-piece on. Classy head-scarf and a very expensive pair of shoes. Crocodile skin. Not mock-croc.

I don't look up ladies' clothes very well.

I mean that I don't look well in ladies' clothes.

No! I'm not up very much when I see ladies with no clothes.

Damn!

I'm not very well up in ladies' clothes. That's what I mean to say. But I guess that she represents about two hundred and fifty pounds on the hoof. Sorry, probably only thinks in guineas.

So do I, but I'm a pig.

(Publisher's Note: Oh, dear. Must have dropped off there for a minute. Why is Mister May calling himself a pig, though I wouldn't be the one to argue? I never believe in getting all worked up.)

A guinea-pig, you silly Publisher!

Perhaps you alert readers, which means all of you, will have spotted that yet again he has given himself away. Note the words 'I never believe in getting all worked up.'

And so says his poor wife.

'Can I help you?'

In case you might have forgotten in all those interruptions, it is the lovely lady whose appliance I have come to service, still there on the doorstep.

'Gas Board.'

She looks me up and down with that sort of look that makes Edgar swell with pride.

'Mama will be pleased to see you.'

'She's been having trouble, has she?'

'That's one way of putting it.'

'Well, I know lots of different ways of putting it,' I say, not to be outdone in the wicked words game.

'Well, well. A witty gasman. That *is* a surprise. Mama'll be even more pleased. Come in.'

I come in.

You mustn't get the impression that the house contains some beautiful and valuable things. Pictures and antiques. I'm sure that if you went to the British Museum and the Victoria and Albert Museum you'd find things at least half as nice.

The girl, who tells me that her name is Dorothea Fleetfoot, leads me upstairs to a kitchen. Honest. Some people actually do have their kitchens upstairs. Be a good idea for my old mum. Not so far for the smell of burning to rise.

Some readers have written to me and complained that I shouldn't make jokes about my mum's cooking, and that she can't be as bad as I pretend.

She can.

She is.

I remember the time that she makes some biscuits for my old man and they're so hard that he can't even crack them with the coal hammer.

So what does my mum do? Goes round to the grocer and complains that he's sold her some tough flour!

The kitchen contains enough equipment to make even a gourmet gallop. But Dorothea leads me past there to a sitting-room with a fabulous big sofa in it. The curtains are drawn and the only light comes from a standard lamp near the door.

'Would you like to lie down on there, Mister . . . ?'

'I'm May.'

(Publisher's Note: Nooooooooooooooooooo!!!!!!!)

Yes.

'Of course you may. But I didn't catch the name.'

'I didn't throw it to you. I'm Jonny May.'

'Really.' Again the up and down look. 'Excellent. Really

jolly super. Mama will be so delighted.'

'Why?'

'Oh.' The question seems not to have occurred to her and she stands thinking, her hand rubbing an imaginary crease in her faultless skirt.

'Why will she be so pleased with me?'

'Because of what you're here to do.'

'For the Gas.'

'Of course. Now you will be good?'

'Dorothea, I shall be sensational.'

We both laugh. Then the words that spilled from her dainty mouth a half page back impact on my mind.

'Lie down on the sofa!!'

'Yes. Mama complains that when she lies down on the sofa there for her afternoon siesta, she smells this frightful pong of gas. So if you could lie down in the same place, perhaps you might be able to trace it.'

'On the sofa?'

'On the sofa.'

'There.'

She pushes me in the chest and I topple backwards faster than a snail on ice. Simultaneously, as well as at the same time, the light goes off.

'What?'

'Nothing.'

'Who?'

'Me, Jonathan.'

'Where?'

'Here.'

'When?'

'Now?'

'Why?'

'Because I like you.'

'How?'

'Like this.'

'This' involves me losing my clothes faster than I would have believed possible. It seems almost as if there are two pairs of hands stripping me. She may be called 'Fleetfoot' but she is very fleet of finger. I am amazed at her cunning, for I obtain the curious illusion that Edgar is being given a thorough massage at the same time that someone is pulling my New Riders of the Purple Sage t-shirt over my head.

It's the darkness that makes me lose my senses.

'Dorothea?'

'I'm here.'

I am lying naked on my back on this well-padded sofa, on well-stuffed cushions, in a warm dark room. And on top of me there is lying a warm bird, who is very well-padded and is about to be well-stuffed. Before you can say: 'Whipped cream is masochistic milk', Edgar is home and wet, feeling as snug as a bug in a rug.

Dorothea is running her finger gently as a feather around my lips, finally letting me suck it into my mouth. I bite it hard. Hard enough for her to feel but not hard enough to cripple, and am rewarded by feeling her hips jerk and a certain tightening of muscles that some ladies sadly don't even realise that they've got.

'Oooh.'

'Nice?'

'Very, Jonny. You weren't boasting. You're really very sensational.'

'Oh.'

That's me when Edgar is suddenly pulled out of the warmth and starts feeling the cold. But there is a lot of shuffling and fumbling in the darkness and I open my mouth to complain that I am not being attended to.

When Edgar finds that Dorothea is a true lady, who is prepared to put her mouth where her . . . whatever the saying is.

My complaint is stifled. One possibility to explain the sensation I feel is that I am being kissed by a very big man with fat cheeks and a large moustache.

There are at least sixty-nine other answers, but I find that I quickly get to the bottom of the mystery.

The answer is handed to me on a plate, though I am only prepared to pay it lip-service.

I am considering sending that little bit of narration to the *Guinness Book of Records* as having the most double meanings to a line than anything since Max Miller last played the Aston Hippodrome. And won.

'Which way do you want it, Jonny?' I hear a voice whispering from the blackness, and Edgar feels a touch of the shivers for a moment.

'Any way you like.'

What an English gentleman!

'I think I'd like to do it properly for the first time, and then we'll see.'

Dorothea has such confidence. 'The *first* time.' I will do my best not to disappoint her.

'What about your Mama?'

The movement stops and the room seems to have grown a touch chilly.

'What do you . . . what do you mean, Jonny?'

'I just thought that you mentioned about your mother being pleased I had come.'

'You haven't! And I never noticed. That is rather beastly of you.'

'No. I mean *come* to your house.'

'Oh that. My Mama isn't going to like that.'

In true music-hall fashion I give her the immortal reply: 'Your Mama isn't going to get it.'

Funny. Usually gets a giggle from the ladies. Maybe Dorothea is low on humour.

I let the thought slide as things are beginning to happen which call for all of my attention. Pardon me, friends, for a moment.

'Aaaaaah!'

'Oooooh!'

One is me and the other is Dorothea but I'm damned if I can tell which is which in the heat of the moment.

Before I've regained my breath poor old Edgar is out in the cold yet again, and I hear feet pattering softly over the carpet. I remember that unfortunate business of Aunt Rose and the Scottish football supporter, but I hardly think that Miss Fleetfoot is the sort of person who is going to start selling tickets for the Jonny May Ball.

I lie there for a few moments in total darkness getting myself together and wondering if Dorothea is going to come back for another bite at the cherry. When the door opens and I catch a swift glance of a female figure silhouetted against the light from the hall.

Then there is the pattering of feet towards me, and hands brushing over the business end of the May anatomy. There is a short sigh or two from the dimness. And then I am ready to be tried on for sighs.

I make a grab for the body I can only sense near to me. With a classy bird like Dorothea it is certainly not common sense. Again there is a muffled gasp as my fingers come into contact with what might be a caramel cream topped with a grape, but isn't.

'Which way this time, Dorothea?' I ask, not knowing if she fancies a new angle.

A mathematically inclined young lady I once know tells me that the angle of dangle is inversely proportional to the throb of the knob, all other things remaining equal.

There is no reply to my question, but I am heaved around on the sofa like a sack of best nuts. The Sloane Square Miss was well endowed to start with, but all the passionate exercise seems to have made her bust out all over. There feels to be rather more of her than there was before. But this is clearly a trick of the light. Or dark.

For once I find that we are about to do it in the conventional position. The missionary one. So named because all of those randy missionaries used to lay the native birds and this was the only way they knew, having lead cloistered lives. Like those monks with their dirty habits.

Apart from the seeming difference in upper measurement, Dorothea has also become . . . I don't know quite how to put it.

Not 'it', darling.

She's not quite as . . . well, sort of, snugly fitting as she was. I know that the May masher is highly regarded as a most formidable weapon, but I've never known it actually *stretch* anyone before. It's quite frightening that I have such a fearsome power. I must watch it carefully. Might do somebody a real injury with it.

I don't want to give the impression that Dorothea has turned in mid-stroke to a reasonable facsimile of the Blackwall Tunnel, or anything like that. It's just that she had a really tight aperture, to use a camera expression. Now she's gone a bit out of focus.

Doesn't interfere with my enjoyment of the situation and I am able to bring myself to the edge and look over in a good average time.

'Bet your Mama wouldn't mind this,' I grunt between strokes.

There is no reply.

When Miss Fleetfoot finally joins me on the edge and leaps over holding hands, not unlike Butch and Sundance, apart from us not shouting out that rude word like they do, she shows yet another peculiar change. Before it was a single very explosive outburst, like a starshell exploding up in the wide blue yonder.

This time it's more like a string of fire-crackers, banging off one after another. I guess there are at least eight or ten separate small shudders, each of which Edgar enjoys immensely. Followed by one larger explosion.

'Ooh!'

'Ooh!'

They both sound the same so I won't bother to tell you which is me and which is Dorothea.

'Finished?'

My goodness! That's amazing. Dorothea has the ability to throw her voice. Though she's still with me, and we are still closely connected, her voice floats from over by the door.

The light comes on.

By thc door.

Switched on by Dorothea.

By Double and Trouble! I know, and Edgar knows, that she cannot be in two places at once. Yet she is still under me, *and* over there.

'All right, Mama?'

'All right, darling. He was lovely.'

The first voice comes from over by the door and the second from the sofa.

'Mama!!!!!!!!!'

'Yes, Jonny, isn't it? But I think you should really call me Mrs Fleetfoot as we haven't yet been formally introduced to each other.'

I've been had.

Not once but twice. That's why there's the difference between them, here and there. It explains the darkness. And I said that Mama wouldn't like it. How very wrong I was.

Mama is a very attractive lady in her mid-forties, and well preserved. I don't mind too much, specially as I get a bonus for my double and quits performance which will go towards the Jonathan May fund for hard times.

Only one thing sends a bit of a shudder down my spine. As they are showing me out, Mama smiles benevolently at me, like an absconding bishop, and says! 'How nice to have had you, Jonathan. What a pity Granny wasn't here.'

Chapter Twelve

The demonstration is very near. In fact it's this afternoon at the main hall of the Gas offices. Mandy Ranndee and I have been through it over and over again until we could do it in our sleep. For the last time I tell you that I am not talking about doing 'it' with Miss Ranndee, though I still have very high hopes. As far as she's concerned my hopes are the only things that she allows to get raised while she's around.

Before I plunge in and tell you about it, I promised you a joke about a famous footballer in the last chapter. As this is likely to be the last chapter, I might as well tell it to you now.

Like I said, I was told this one about a certain international footballer who is the Best. But I don't for one split second believe that. Funnily enough, I have a cousin named Terry, who once plays a few times for West Brom. Fancies himself as one of the great soccer stars of all time. He's about as modest as Stan Bowles and Rodney and Mac rolled into one.

This time that I'm telling you about, Cousin Terry is in bed with this sexy chick he goes around with called Jane. But he's boring her, and I don't mean into holes.

He reaches over and gets her to put her fingers on his forehead. 'Feel that?'

'Yeah. What about it?'

'I bet you've never felt anything like that before. That has scored more goals this season than any other head in the entire country.'

Minute later he wriggles around and gets her to hold his right foot. 'Bet you never felt anything like that before?' he says.

'What about it?' asks Jane.

'Well, that foot has scored more goals this season than any other right foot in British football.'

By now Jane is really fed up with his boasting and she decides to get her own back, so she grabs his hand and places it right smack-bang in . . . in the middle of . . . her love lay-by.

'There, Terry. I bet *you* never felt anything like that before, did you?'

He doesn't move his hand, just lying there, thinking about it. After a half a minute he sits upright. 'Funnily enough, I have done,' he says. 'I felt just like that when I missed that penalty against Chelsea last week!'

'I want you two to perform for us. For the Gas Board. For your own country. For your families. For yourselves. For the people of Britain.'

Mister Weeny is getting so worked up over his big speech to Mandy and me that I can almost hear the faint strains of 'Land of Pope And Tory' floating in my ears, and I am forced to wipe away a quite imaginary tear.

'Behave with dignity. Work well and hard. Hold fast to that which is true. Render to no man evil for evil. Strengthen the faint-hearted.'

Now it's like our old Chief Master at the beginning of a new term.

'Dignity. Honesty. Brevity. Efficiency. And let us not forget sanctity.'

I haven't forgotten sanctity. To be quite honest I always thought that sanctity meant a French lady with five Bristols.

He shakes me by the hand and plants several kisses on Miss

Ranndee's cheeks. I am delighted that he didn't get us mixed up.

I will fill you in on the details of what Miss Ranndee and I are supposed to be doing this fine sunny afternoon. Not the most difficult of tasks, even for someone like me. I can't answer for Mandy.

A grandstand has been erected along one side of the hall with about eighty seats for the ladies and gentlemen of the Press. Each with their own notebook and their own little gas jet. Complete with their own free lighter to ignite the flame when Mandy and I have done our stuff. And there will certainly be a flame as we are both pretty hot stuff.

Thinking about being hot stuff and about journalists reminds me of something that my old mum mentioned in her last letter from home.

Seems that there was a bit of a do at the local boozer and the local reporters were there in force, lured by the promise of a human interest story.

And free drinks.

My old man, as one of the regulars for many years, is much in demand, and knocks back the free ale like he's got hollow legs. Staggers about until he's confronted by this smashing young bird with gigantic knockers.

She's got a notebook and pencil in her hand and a big sign pinned to her chest that says 'Press'.

My old man does, and his case comes up next week.

Mandy and I march in dressed in gleaming white overalls, and we both pull out our tools, which should make the front pages of some newspapers, and set to in repairing an imaginary leak in a pipe. After a suitable pause for dramatic effect, we will achieve success and the reporters will light their pipes. And cigarettes if they have any.

The walls are covered with slogans.

'High speed gas helps you!'

'Gas is safe and cheap.'

'Great Gas!'

'Gas – the heat you can see!'

'Gas is good for you!'

'Gas meanz heatz!'

I'm sure I've read something like that last one somewhere else.

There's only five minutes to go. I've had a few words with Hairy Harry, who is the fitter that endured Mandy while she was training.

'Don't make any of your sarcastic jokes with her, Jonny,' he says. 'She's got no sense of humour and she'll just take everything at face value. She's carrying a big cylinder the other day and moaning about her boy friend. I tell her to drop it. So she does. Lucky we don't all go up with it.'

I shall remember his advice and not make a single remark that can be misinterpreted.

(Publisher's Note: I can scent trouble coming for Mister May. But I shall do nothing. Just lie back and hope.)

There he goes again. 'I shall do nothing. Just lie back and hope.' That poor wife of his.

The room is beginning to fill up.

'For God's sake make sure the pressure's properly balanced. Ignite it when it's too low and we'll get a suck-back that'll force a great flame out of every jet and set fire to half of the country's top reporters. And it's the sort of accident that can set British Gas back by fifty years. So no stupid mistakes by either of you!'

I don't like the sound of that suck-back that Mister Weeny threatens us with. Very nasty.

But at least he goes and leaves us on our own. I am wearing a very snazzy pair of white overalls, with a suitable slogan on them. 'The best in Gas is the best in Gas.' Like all great slogans it doesn't mean a thing.

Mandy is wearing an ever smarter outfit, and hold on your seat Elias Banglestein, because your very favourite word is coming along in just a moment.

But first, a commercial break.

Keep the letters coming, folks. And lots of jokes. You can see that I need them. And ladies, remember how you can make a young man very happy. Speed along your frillies to me at the Publisher's address at the front of the book. That's Sphere Books, 30–32 Gray's Inn Road, London WC1.

End of commercial break.

That's the shortest break since Ronnie Corbett's little finger.

Miss Ranndee's outfit is calculated to get maximum exposure in the Press. It reveals maximum exposure of Miss Ranndee. A white halter top, that barely contains her two most obvious assets. It gives you some idea of her limited brain-power when I tell you that she has to take her bra off to be able to count to two.

There is a matching white skirt that would make a fine shawl for a fieldmouse. It doesn't even begin to hide the matching white knickers that would make a useful pocket handkerchief for a ladybird. The skirt and knickers qualify for match of the day.

'I'm ever so nervous, Jonny. I just don't know what to do with myself.'

I pat her on the shoulder, which is one of the few parts of her body that are covered up. 'Don't worry, love. Just take yourself in hand.'

I am busy with my own tools, and I look round thirty seconds later to see that she has taken my last instruction literally, and is busy with her own tools.

'Stop it!'

'Why, Jonny?'

'First off anyone might see you.'

'Yes.'

'Second you'll get dirty finger-marks on your clean skirt and knickers.'

'Sorry, Jonny.'

'And thirdly you'll go deaf and blind.'

Mandy stops. The seats are nearly full. I recognise several journalists who often appear on telly. The lady with the cigarette holder and horny-rimmed glasses. Marge Whoops or something. Very sexy lady, I always reckon. And there's that one in the bow tie. Must say I don't find him at all sexy!

Mister Meeny is tapping the microphone as nervously as a candidate for 'New Faces'. The nineteen seventies answer to the Bloody Assizes.

I look at the connection that we are to make, and try and ignore the fact that Mandy is bending over only an inch and a quarter from the end of my nose. If I were to lick my lips now I could end up in court. The white knickers seem to be trying to do an Evel Knievel disappearing dive between the walls of her canyon.

I have made sure that all of my tools are in the best condition possible. Despite not having seen anything from Liz James for so long, though her last card hints that she has had enough of hot porridge and cold kilts, *all* of my tools are in excellent condition.

'My lords, ladies and gentlemen, and a special welcome to our visitors from the Fourth Estate.'

'What does that mean, Jonny? Is that like being given the third degree?'

'No. Fourth Estate means they all play the same sort of games. They'll all fore-players.'

'Oh. You are clever, Jonny. After this is all over, why don't you ask me out for a nibble on a hamburger?'

'I've got a better idea. Why don't you take me in for a nibble on you?'

She puts her head on one side, making herself look like a sexy, short-sighted rabbit. 'Maybe I will, Jonny. You must wait. Everything waits for he who comes.'

I will not argue with that.

But I must carry on taking the greatest care with what I say. The reference to taking herself in hand shows that all too clearly.

Mister Meeny is reaching the end of his speech. And his tether too, by the pale look of apprehension on his face. I guess that he is going through agonies wondering if Mandy is worth all the trouble. For that half hour of fun and laughter in his office, his whole career is going to hang in the balance if she makes a boob. And the way that halter top doesn't fit her properly, I would not be in the least surprised to see a couple of boobs.

But Meeny can relax. Jonny has everything totally under control. Though I am confronted with an impressive array of dials and pipes, I know precisely what the majority of them do.

Nothing.

They're just for show.

I don't know what it is, but there is an odd smell somewhere in the hall. Must be all those journalists packed together. A strange smell. Maybe it's whiskey and cigarettes. But there's a very strict No Smoking rule today. It was all I could do to stop Miss Ranndee from packing her fags in her bag. Though I spot she has left the box of matches there. Still, after all our training, not even Mandy would be silly enough to strike a light.

'And in conclusion, I would now introduce you to the two wonderful young people who have been selected by a series of special tests and examinations for this task.'

Mandy passed her special test as easy as lying flat on your back with your legs in the air. Jonny had to work a bit harder for his.

'The fetching young lady is Miss Mandy Ranndee.'

And we all know what's she's fetching.

'While the young man at her side is Jonathan May. Mandy is from London, while Jonny is from the north. He's a Birmingham lad.'

By Snow and Hill! He doesn't need to tell the world where I come from. I do have my pride.

My Uncle Nick would be spinning in his grave. If he was dead that is. His brother Julian dies a few months ago, up in Brum-land, and he says he wants to be buried at sea.

Terrible business it was.

Six of his mates drowned trying to dig the grave.

The work is moving on smoothly, with Blue Meeny giving a staggering commentary on what we're doing. It would be a running commentary but he's got a bad leg.

I wish I could work out what that funny smell is. And it seems to be getting worse.

So far everything is going as smoothly as a well-greased toboggan. I have taken all precautions, and left not a rolling stone unturned.

The thought of Jagger and Company Unlimited puts me in mind of that song of theirs, and I begin to hum it under my breath.

Mandy is smiling vaguely at me, and shaking it all about for the benefit of the Press as she hands me spanners and wrenches. I don't mind a quick wrench now and again.

That smell is really awful.

'Jonny and Mandy will soon be finished now, and when they do, I'm sure we shall have a nice surprise.'

'Jumping Jack Flash,' I sing.

Horrible smell.

Like . . .

'Jonny?'

'What is it?'

'I can smell something.'

'Jumping Jack Flash,' I still hum under my breath.

'Don't worry, Mandy. Can't be anything. It's very probably a . . .'

'Jumping Jack Flash.'

'It's a . . .'

The penny drops.

'It's gas, gas, GAS!!!!!'

It's all very well old Jonesy going round saying not to panic and how they don't like it up them. I'm on the edge of panic, because I don't want it up me. Or me up with it, as the case might be.

Mandy is on her way out of the hall when I grab her by the back of the skirt. Not easy when you realise how short the skirt is.

'Don't do that! If those reporters think something's wrong then the whole demonstration goes for a James.'

James, as in James Burton, who is about the best country-rock guitarist around, in case you wondered.

She calms down. 'But Jonny. A gas leak. What shall I do? Eh?'

'I'll carry on with what I've got to do, but I'll slow it down. Premature ignition would be even worse than premature evacuation.'

And I bet that's not what you thought I was going to say, was it, Missus?

Mandy goes groping around amid the tangle of wires and pipes. Trouble is, she doesn't know which are real and which are for show. I know, but I have to carry on with the joining up work as she can't do that either. I mutter a swift curse against Mister Weeny.

'Jonny is speeding along there. Just a touch behind schedule, I'm afraid. I shall have to dock his bonus.'

He ought to be in the dock himself. Preferably the dock of the bay.

'I can't find it.'

'Keep looking.' I fear that Mandy would not even be able to find it if she could use both hands.

'I can smell it.'

'So can I. And it's getting worse. Hurry up. Can't light it in case the suck-back sucks back and then we're all in it.'

Actually, the Press will be more in than us. But some of them could do with a bit of livening up.

'I still can't find it.' There is a note of desperation in her hiss. Like a viper with gut-rot. And I am not talking about a vindscreen viper, either.

'Just keep on trying.'

Is my guardian angel deserting me? Will the greatest chance for me to make it with the Gas Board end with a pathetic whimper? As long as it doesn't end with a bang, I don't mind.

'Come on, Jonny and Mandy!' There is a note of desperation in Mister Weeny's voice. He can see his promotion going up in smoke. Not that anything is likely to actually go up in smoke. With Jonathan May in control, the situation will not reach that level of disaster.

'Jonny?'

'What?' As if I didn't know!

'I'm trying.'

'Very!'

'Trying to find that leak. It's getting worse and worse and I can't find it.'

I shall soon lose my cool and become very sarcastic. I can't stand silly birds. Even when they're wearing white knickers and very short skirts.

'Jonny. What shall I do?'

At the same moment Mister Weeny booms out over the loudspeaker: 'I can see that our young hopefuls are making sure that we have the best job possible. Let's not keep the Press waiting too much longer.'

Trouble is, when you write down the words like that it seems all very calm. When you hear Weeny, he sounds like a demented Bay City Roller fan on the farthest edge of hysteria. I haven't heard anyone so near to panic since my old man found mum had used a certain chocolate laxative instead of cooking chocolate on a cake.

Made him feel as if the world had fallen out of his bottom.

Weeny is getting really desperate, and so am I. Which reminds me. Did I ever tell you the definition of desperation? I didn't? Well I will now.

The definition of desperation is someone with a dreadful squitters trying to pick the lock on a lavatory with a piece of wet string.

I have done everything I can and there is a limit to the amount of time you can spend on useless fiddling. Even Nero learned that. The smell of gas is unbelievably strong now, and I am surprised that nobody else can smell it.

'Jonny?'

'What is it? I am thoroughly kissed off with Miss Ranndee by now, and not even the thought of those tight little knickers embracing the exciting rumpo makes a difference.

'What shall I do to find the leak?'

'What do you think?' I say, my sarcasm blanking out my common-sense. 'Light a match and go and look for it.'

The moment I've said that I realise that I have made a ghastly mistake. But it is too late.

'Light a match, Jonny? All ri . . .'

BOOOOOOOOOOOOOOOOOOOOOOOOM

Nobody actually gets killed. A few forelocks get singed. And hairpieces and eyebrows vanish in smoke. I take the opportunity to also vanish in the smoke.

I hear nothing ever again from Mister Weeny or from Mandy Ranndee.

So it's over. Another job gone. I can't understand it. I try. I really do.

Still, there's bad news and good news. This book might be over, but Liz James is coming back from Scotland. And I have a pound or two salted away. So life isn't too miserable.

Thanks for reading. Keep looking out for what happens when Liz gets back. I might even try and get another job.

Until then, I'll leave you with a littlc good news – bad news joke.

My Uncle Angus gets shipwrecked in the Pacific during the War and cast up alone on a rocky island. Where he meets this character with a long beard and long hair, who tells him that he's been on this island for a year.

'And,' he goes on, 'I have bad news and good news for you.'

'What's the bad news?' says Uncle Angus.

'There's nothing at all to eat except bird droppings.'

'Oh, that's awful,' says Uncle Angus. 'But what's the good news?'

'Ah,' says the castaway. 'The good news is that there's plenty of it.'

Evening all.

Hilarious Fiction from Sphere

CONFESSIONS FROM A SEX CLINIC

Jonathan May

Miss Thrustinne's Sex Clinic for repressed gentlewomen seems to provide Jonny's ideal niche in life, and very niche it is too. The new position has plenty of openings for an enterprising young man. Surely Jonny is the very chap to wave his magic wand (not that he's a good fairy) and solve the personal problems of these distressed ladies? Jonny is certainly prepared to put all he's got into the work. He's all set to spend the rest of his active life up to his ears (so to speak) in his favourite position. But trust him to get caught in flagrante delicto – that's Spanish for 'with his trousers in the vicinity of his ankles.' Only Jonny could blow his prospects in such a spectacular fashion!

59838 60p

Sphere Books Present

UNDER THE DOCTOR

Peter Buchanan

Dr Boyd is a psychiatrist popular with female patients who discuss their sexual problems with him. Three visit him in turn. Marian yearns to make love with a complete stranger because an incident with her stepfather in her early teens stops her from fancying anyone she knows. Dr Boyd tells her to fantasise the perfect cure – and her fantasy is all about him!
Lady Victoria is bored with her jetset life which is financed by money she has conned from her many lovers. Her father wants her to marry wealthy Rodney but she prefers the uncouth butler Wilkins. Dr Boyd tells her to fantasise the perfect solution to her dilemma – and her fantasy is all about him! The third patient, Sandra, already lives in a fantasy world in which she is married to a highly-sexed husband. In fact she isn't married at all, but she dreams of having a husband who is not so easily turned on and who needs to be seduced by her – and her dreams are all about Dr Boyd!

A hilarious screen romp starring Barry Evans, Liz Fraser and Hilary Pritchard.

20354 65p.

Film Tie-in Available from Sphere Books

HARDCORE

Fiona Richmond

Fiona Richmond is a vicar's daughter who first tasted the delights of love with a veterinary surgeon, a chemistry master and a French air hostess (though not of course, all together!) And that was just the start!

Now the full story of Fiona's erotic exploits is at last revealed. Here are the adventures – in and out of the bedroom – that led to her fame and fortune. And these adventures make Fanny Hill look like Little Bo Peep! First there was the impresario who gave her two minutes to impress him – he's still recovering. Then there was the television director who monitored everything – but *everything*. And the elegant Lord who insisted on discipline before dinner. And then – well, read on . . . !

HARDCORE is now a major film starring *Fiona Richmond* and *Anthony Steele*.

35645 65p